'Please. I'm not into games. Exactly what is it you want from me?'

The humour faded from his eyes in an instant, replaced by a brooding severity she hadn't seen before. It caught her by surprise.

So did his hand, reaching out and enfolding hers. His touch was light but firm, his flesh warm and enticing. She sucked in a breath.

'Exactly?' His thumb stroked over hers, sending a shiver of excitement straight to her secret feminine core.

'I would like to know you better, Rosalie. *Much better.*' Another stroke of his thumb made her tremble. 'I want to become your lover.'

**Annie West** spent her childhood with her nose between the covers of a book—a habit she retains. After years preparing government reports and official correspondence she decided to write something she *really* enjoys. And there's nothing she loves more than a great romance. Despite her office-bound past, she has managed a few interesting moments—including a marriage offer with the promise of a herd of camels to sweeten the contract. She is happily married to her ever-patient husband (who has never owned a dromedary). They live with their two children amongst the tall eucalypts at beautiful Lake Macquarie, on Australia's east coast. You can e-mail Annie at www.annie-west.com

# FOR THE SHEIKH'S PLEASURE

BY
ANNIE WEST

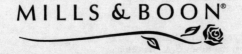

MILLS & BOON®

First published in Great Britain 2007
Harlequin Mills & Boon Limited,
Eton House, 18-24 Paradise Road, Richmond, Surrey TW9 1SR

© Annie West 2007

ISBN-13: 978 0 263 85343 8

Set in Times Roman 10½ on 12 pt
01-0807-54337

Printed and bound in Spain
by Litografia Rosés, S.A., Barcelona

# FOR THE SHEIKH'S PLEASURE

To my friend Vanessa: a talented writer and a girl who knows the value of best-quality chocolate. Thanks for the unexpected supply that powered this story.
I owe you!

# CHAPTER ONE

THERE she was.

Arik adjusted the binoculars a fraction to bring her into clearer focus.

A slow smile stretched his mouth as the early light limned her figure with gold.

Surprising to realise how disappointed he'd been just moments ago, thinking she wouldn't arrive. She'd become the highlight of each tedious day as she appeared on the beach, a lone, perfect Aphrodite with her long rippling hair, her delicious curves and her air of innocent allure.

Even at a distance of five hundred metres, the sight of her tightened each muscle in his lower body, turned his blood sluggish as his heartbeat slowed to a heavy anticipatory thud.

He lowered the binoculars and scrubbed his hand over his face.

Hell! What had he come to? Six weeks in plaster and he was reduced to playing the voyeur. Maybe he should have accepted one of the offers of feminine companionship he'd received while he recuperated.

But he'd been impatient to get this leg healed. He didn't want any fawning women around, fussing over him and nurturing false hopes of domestic bliss, staying here in his home. He'd seen the look in Helene's eyes just a couple of months ago and had known immediately it was time to end their relationship.

A pity. Helene was clever and witty, as well as sleekly seductive and with an appetite for sex he found rare in a woman. Their time together had been stimulating, satisfying and fun. But once she'd started dreaming about happily-ever-after, it was over.

He worked hard and played hard, seeking out women who'd enjoy the fast-paced ride with him. He wasn't into breaking hearts.

No, what he needed now was a diversion, a short, satisfying affair that would keep his mind off the frustration of being cooped up here.

He lifted the binoculars again and was rewarded with a sight that made him lean forward, elbows braced on the parapet.

His golden girl had put up her easel, positioned for the view along the beach to the next rocky headland. But, instead of concentrating on her paints, she was unbuttoning her shirt.

Arik's heart jolted in expectation. Yes! Her hands skimmed quickly down the shirt, then she shrugged it off, revealing smooth shoulders and arms and a curvaceous body that made him want to discard the wheelchair and hobble down to help her undress. Slim at the waist but full-breasted: she'd be a delicious handful, he decided as he watched her bend to strip off her trousers. A ripe peach of a *derrière*, invitingly curved hips and slim shapely legs.

Just as he'd suspected. A woman worth knowing better.

He watched her walk down to the waves curling in on the sand. Saw her pause as the water frothed about her ankles. It would be warm, caressing her skin. The current in this part of the Arabian Sea kept the temperature inviting.

His gaze roved appreciatively down her back, her legs and up again to the swell of her breasts as she turned. Abruptly her chin lifted and she stared straight up at him, as if she could make him out among the shadows on the long terrace.

A *frisson* of something shot through him.

Recognition? No, that was impossible.

And yet the illusion that their eyes met and held for one, two, three long pulse beats was strong enough to jerk him out of his complacent speculation.

He lowered the glasses and stared at her. But already she'd turned away, stepping out into the shallows till the waves lapped around her dark one-piece swimsuit.

She'd look better in a bikini.

Or best of all, nude.

He watched as she waded out further, then, with a sinuous shallow dive, swam out with an easy stroke into the bay. He leaned back in his seat, relieved to see she was clearly at home in the water. There'd be no need for any emergency rescue.

She swam for twenty minutes then waded ashore. The first rosy light of dawn had dissipated as the sun rose higher and brighter. It lit her to perfection, slanting off a body that made him itch to be rid of the full-leg plaster and down on the sand beside her. Close. Touching. Learning the texture of those smooth limbs, her scent, the taste of her skin against his lips, the sound of her sighs as she surrendered to pleasure.

Heat roared through him, a blaze of wanting so strong he shifted in his seat, fully aroused and impatient that he couldn't get what he wanted immediately.

If they'd been alive a hundred years ago, he could have snapped his fingers and had her brought instantly before him. It was a shame some of the old ways had died. There were definite drawbacks to the march of progress. To being a civilised man. Especially when there was something utterly *un*civilised about the feelings this woman sparked in him.

Who was she? Where was she from? With that long swathe of blonde hair she was no local.

He leaned back in the chair as he contemplated the possibilities.

A girl: gorgeous, alone, tempting.

A man: bored, frustrated and intrigued.

Another smile curved his lips. He wasn't the sort to sit and wonder. He was all for action and that was exactly what he planned to get.

Soon—very soon—he'd satisfy his curiosity about her. And more…

Rosalie tucked her hair behind her ear and critically surveyed her landscape. After days of effort she'd made pathetically little progress. Despite every attempt, the scene still eluded her. She'd sketched the outline of beach and headland, attempted a watercolour and toyed with oils. But nothing had worked. Nor had the photos she'd taken captured the spirit of the place, the sheer magic of it.

The translucent ripple of the early morning tide, the impossible blush-pink of the fine-grained sand marking the long crescent of beach, the sheer vertical drop of the blue-shadowed headland, like a brooding sentinel. And the Moorish fantasy of angled walls, perfect arches and deep terraces that comprised the ancient ochre-coloured fort dominating the cliff line.

From the first morning she'd rounded the point and discovered this bay, she'd felt the unfamiliar fizz of excitement, of anticipation in her veins. It had taken her by surprise. A sensation she'd never thought to experience again.

The stark beauty of the place had made her long to paint once more. And surely it was inspirational enough to reawaken her long-neglected talent, coax and inspire her into achieving something at least passably encouraging.

It had given her the courage to open the art supplies her mother had smuggled hopefully into the luggage.

But years of inactivity had taken their toll. Whatever artistic talent Rosalie had once aspired to, it would clearly take more than this spectacular scene to reawaken it.

Perhaps she'd lost it for ever—that joyous gift of translating what she saw into something worth keeping on canvas.

Three years ago she'd accepted the loss with a sullen stoicism. It hadn't even distressed her, given the fact that her whole world had shattered around her. Three years ago she hadn't *wanted* to paint any more. It had been left to her family and friends to fret over the change in her.

But now, to her surprise, something, a tentative hope, a flutter of excitement, had flared into life. Only to be extinguished by disappointing reality.

She ripped the page from her sketchbook in disgust. There was something missing.

Her lips curved in a cynical smile. *Talent, obviously*.

But something else too, she realised as she scrutinised the view. Despite the rolling surge of waves on the shore and the slow whirl of a falcon high over the cliff ahead, the scene lacked life.

She stood and stretched her cramped muscles.

It didn't matter. She couldn't do it justice anyway.

She was no artist. Not any more. She firmed her lips to counter the sudden absurd wobble of her chin as devastation rocked her.

Stupid, stupid, to even hope to regain what she'd lost. That part of her life had gone for ever.

She sucked in a deep sustaining breath. She was a survivor, she'd dragged herself out of fear and fury and grief and got on with living. More than that, she'd found peace and joy in her new life. A happiness she'd never thought to experience. She was a lucky woman. What did it matter if she'd never be an artist?

But her hands trembled as she gathered her gear, carefully stowed each item in her bag. Somehow the truth was harder to bear now after that brief surge of hope and inspiration.

She wouldn't walk this way again and torture herself with what she couldn't have. Instead she'd concentrate on other things. Sightseeing in the quaint old coastal town with its souk and its minarets. Maybe take a trip into the desert. Get back into swimming each day and finally open the paperback mystery she'd brought on her holiday.

She'd forget the haunting beauty of the deserted bay and its *Arabian Nights* fortress.

Her bag was almost packed when something, some distant sound or flash of motion, made her look up.

At the far end of the beach something moved. Something that resolved itself into two shapes, white-gold in the early light. Shapes that moved towards her with a steady pace, then plunged suddenly towards the sea.

Rosalie stared, recognising the beasts now. How could she not, since her brother-in-law was an enthusiastic breeder of horses? These two weren't just any horses; they were Arabs, finely proportioned with arched elegant necks and a sure gait. A colour somewhere between palest dove-grey and white, she decided as they approached, dancing a little as a wave coursed in around their hooves.

She heard a whinny and saw one toss a long mane. The man on its back leaned forward as if speaking to it, his dark hair ebony against the equine paleness. She saw the horse's ear flicker back, its head turn a fraction.

It was hard to tell where man ended and beast began. He wore white: trousers and a loose long-sleeved shirt, the neck open to reveal a V of dark bronzed skin. There was no saddle and he sat with the easy grace of one who'd grown up on horseback. His powerful shoulders and long frame seemed at odds with the lazy grace of his hands—one on the reins and one holding the second horse's lead.

Without any perceptible direction from the rider, both horses wheeled as one and picked their way through the shallows towards deeper water.

By the time they were fetlock-deep, Rosalie had her sketch-book in her hands, automatically following the graceful curve of necks and powerful haunches, such a contrast to the lean hard lines of the man with them. He was in profile now and for an instant her hand faltered at the pure masculine beauty of him. Too far away to read the details of his face, but even from here there was something arresting about the tilt of his head, the angle of his nose, the long, burnished column of his throat.

Her heart beat faster as she stared, imprinting impressions on her mind as her hand flew across the paper, desperate to get down the sense of what she saw.

And while she focused on the trio, now deep in the water, she realised that this was precisely what she'd needed to complete the wider landscape. Something living, vibrant and beautiful to breathe energy into the scene.

Over the rush of the waves another sound reached her— the man's deep voice, murmuring what could only be Arabic endearments. The sound rippled across the water and right down into her chest, creating the oddest sensation of loosening warmth deep within her. Then he laughed, a low sound, rich as dark chocolate, and the hairs on the back of her neck stood on end. She shivered, aware of the tightening of her muscles and sudden tension in her spine. But she dismissed it and sketched faster.

Too soon they turned and headed back to shore. They'd be gone before she had a chance to capture even part of what she was trying to achieve.

Frantically Rosalie hunched over her work, trying to catch something of the bond between rider and animal that made them move as one.

It took a few moments to realise they'd turned towards her rather than back the way they'd come.

Details caught her attention as they approached: the faint jingle of harness, the flare of equine nostrils as the horses scented her, the quickening pace, the rider's bare feet, strong and well-shaped. And the way his sodden trousers clung to him, revealing long muscled thighs; even his thin cotton shirt had been liberally splashed, become translucent in places where it caught his skin. Hard planes, flat belly, a ridge of muscle.

Rosalie stopped sketching and lifted her gaze higher.

He was watching her. His eyes were narrowed a little against the angle of the sun but she could see they were liquid-dark and piercing. She sat straighter, barely aware of her rapidly thumping heart. She must have got carried away by the excitement of working again.

But as she met his look she wondered, just for an instant, if it was artistic fervour that notched up her pulse, or something else.

Impossible. Her mouth pinched automatically. There *was* no other explanation. Not for her.

Nevertheless, she couldn't deny he had the sort of face any woman would love to look at. Or any artist.

His body was supple yet powerful. He looked to be around thirty, a study in latent vitality. The breeze ruffled his hair, making it spring with the hint of a curl. His face was long and lean, with exotic, high cut cheekbones. His nose, slightly aquiline, spoke of power and energy, but those angled brows and hooded eyes belonged in a bedroom.

Hastily she looked away, reaching down to pick up the crayon that had fallen to the ground.

Perhaps he was angry that she'd taken his likeness. She hadn't thought of that. She had no idea how the locals would react to her work. Now she wondered about Q'aroumi protocols—whether she should have asked permission first.

She felt the intensity of his regard even while she fumbled in the sand.

'Saba'a alkair.' His voice was low and even more attractive up close.

'Saba'a alkair,' she replied, thankful that she at least knew

how to say good morning in Arabic. 'I hope you don't mind…'
She gestured to the pad before her and then realised, flustered,
that he might not understand her. 'Do you speak—?'

'I speak English,' he answered before she completed the
question. 'You like our scenery?'

Rosalie nodded, tilting her head up to meet his scrutiny and
unable to look away. His eyes were so dark she couldn't dis-
tinguish iris from pupil. It must be a trick of the early morning
light. Close up she knew his eyes must be dark brown, but
from here the illusion was of lustrous, fathomless black. She
hadn't realised it could be so enticing.

'The view from here, it's spectacular.' Her voice was high
and breathless. She strove to control it. 'In the morning light
it's perfect.'

'You will show me your work?' His voice had the faintest
trace of an accent, softening the consonants. Rosalie felt a
shimmer of response deep inside her to its cadence.

An instant later she registered the fact that his question had
sounded more like an order, for all it was softly spoken.

'Am I trespassing?'

He shook his head and she noticed the way his black hair,
slightly long at the back, brushed and curled over his collar.
Even his hair was invested with an aura of vibrancy.

'What would you do if I said you were?' His mouth lifted
up at one side in a half-smile that tugged at something deep
inside her.

'I'd leave, of course.'

Which was exactly what she should do anyway. She
couldn't understand her hypersensitivity to this man. It was
unprecedented. Unsettling.

She got to her feet, stumbling a little as she caught her
balance after sitting engrossed in her drawing.

'Then it's a good thing you're not trespassing.' The half-smile
widened and Rosalie stood, transfixed for a moment by the ef-

fect. Who'd have thought a man with all that power and…yes, authority in his features, could look so charming and—?

'Nevertheless, I should be on my way.'

'Without letting me see your work?'

It would be churlish to refuse. And though her scribbling was nothing like the work she'd once achieved it would be no worse than that of a raw beginner.

She took a step towards him, then paused, unsure of those two horses. This close they looked large and spirited, as if they might shy or, worse, bite.

'No need to fear. Layla and Soraya have excellent manners. They bite no one, not even the hand that feeds them.'

'And that's you?' she asked as she edged closer.

'It is. But that's only one of the reasons they love me, isn't it, my sweets?' He leaned down as he spoke and the horses whickered in response. Then he urged his mount forward and suddenly Rosalie found herself surrounded, a mare on either side. Warmth engulfed her. A damp horsey smell that was somehow earthy and comforting. And something else, less tangible, that teased her nostrils. It intensified as he reached towards her sketch-book. Tangy, salt and spice: the scent of man.

Rosalie's nostrils flared and she took a step back, bumping into a horse. She looked up and met his hooded eyes. The gleam she read there disturbed her.

'Show me?' he murmured and again she felt his voice slip like a velvet ribbon across her skin. She frowned, uneasy and suddenly tense.

'Of course.' *Concentrate on the sketches.* Easier said than done when she was hemmed in, increasingly aware of…something. Something about him that jolted her out of her comfort zone.

She lifted the large sketch-book and flipped over a few pages. What she saw there arrested her, banishing unease and doubt in an instant. The first sketch, of the horses heading into the water, was raw, rough and spare but it caught precisely the effect she'd sought: their elegance of movement and proud bearing.

Without waiting for him to comment, she slid her hand under the page and flipped it over. Another sketch—that distinctive arch of the neck, the wide nostrils and dark eyes. Alive, real, better than anything she'd done in all these days of trying. Another sketch—a blur, a fleeting yet effective impression of movement and another, of horse and man moving centaur-like out of the water.

She caught her breath.

'You're very talented,' he said above her and she was so stunned by what she saw that she said nothing, only turned another page, to find herself staring at hands, his hands, long and square-knuckled and strong. The sharp outline of masculine shoulder, a hint of corded neck and decisive chin and, in the background, a couple of lines that somehow gave the impression of the castle on the hill.

'*Very* talented,' he said, breaking her absorption.

'Thank you.' In her surprise at what she'd produced Rosalie forgot to avoid his gaze and found herself looking up into the dark abyss of his stare. Even this close his eyes were black. How near would she need to be to discern their true colour?

'You don't mind me sketching you? The horses are so beautiful I couldn't resist.'

He leaned closer and she swallowed hard, wondering what was going on behind those unreadable eyes. That was no casual glance. It looked…assessing.

'I'm honoured you chose Layla and Soraya as your subjects.' Arik forbore to mention the drawings of himself. She looked skittish enough already, eyes wide and dazed as if she'd never seen a man before. Yet those sketches confirmed she knew how a man was made. Surely that appreciation of form and detail meant she had a strong sensual awareness.

Instantly anticipation fired his blood and he had to concentrate on schooling his expression to one of mild interest.

His first glance at her this morning had left him disappointed. She'd looked so young—far too young for what he had in mind. But as he'd ridden closer he'd been relieved to find her air of fragility wasn't due to extreme youth, though she had to be only in her early twenties. There was a firmness around her lush mouth, and more, a gravity in her eyes that told him she was no innocent.

His relief had been a physical force, washing over him in a wave that eased the tension in his shoulders.

'Do you prefer landscapes or living subjects?'

The way her eyes darted down to his torso, his hands on the reins, gave him all the answer he wanted, and an idea.

'I…both.' She closed the large pad and turned away, pretending to concentrate on Soraya, who was snuffling at her sleeve in hopes of a treat. But Arik saw the furtive glance his golden girl sent him from under lowered lids. How could he not when she had eyes as mysterious as smoke on water, a green-grey at once enticing and secretive? He felt that glance with the keenness of a blade, sharp and sure against his flesh.

He wanted to vault down to stand beside her. Close enough to enfold her in his arms and feel her warmth.

But, he admitted to himself, he was too proud. If he dismounted his stiff leg would mean he'd have trouble remounting again. He probably shouldn't be riding at all, not yet, but he hadn't been able to resist the temptation to meet her at last, no matter what the doctor's warnings.

He'd already noted her bare ring finger but it made sense to be sure. 'You're here on holiday?'

Slowly she nodded and then turned to stuff the portfolio into a capacious bag. 'Yes.'

'And your husband doesn't mind you venturing out alone?' If she were his he'd keep her close, knowing that with those stunning looks she'd be a magnet for any male not on his deathbed.

She paused, her hands gripping the bag so tightly he saw her knuckles whiten. 'I don't have a husband.' Her voice sounded muffled and he recognised strong emotion in her tone. A disagreement with the boyfriend about long term commitment? Disappointment seared through him.

'Your significant other, then. He doesn't mind?'

She straightened and jammed her fists on to her hips. Her eyes flashed green fire and he realised he'd hit a nerve.

'Your English is excellent.' It was almost an accusation.

'Thank you,' he said, watching her intently.

Eventually she shrugged and her gaze slid away. 'There is no man to object to anything I do.' There was something in her voice, a bitterness that caught his attention. 'I suppose that's unusual in a country like Q'aroum?'

'You may be surprised to learn how independent Q'aroumi women are.' His own mother was a case in point.

He smiled and saw with satisfaction that the attraction was definitely *not* one-sided. So all he had to do was give her the opportunity and soon he'd be enjoying the delights of her warm, willing body. Yet something about her air of caution, as if she were ready to flee at the slightest provocation, tempered his impatience.

'I will look forward to seeing you another morning.' He made as if to pull on the reins.

'You'll be back here tomorrow?' Her eyes were bright, her tone a shade too eager. It told him all he needed to know.

He shrugged. 'I hadn't planned to come here.' He paused, as if considering. 'You want to see the horses again? Is that it? You wish to draw them?'

She nodded. 'If you don't mind. That would be wonderful. I'd like…' She bit her lip and he silently urged her to continue. 'I'd like to paint the scene with them here. If it's possible.'

Taking candy from a baby. 'I suppose that can be arranged,' he said after making her wait a few moments. 'I could ask old Ahmed to bring them.'

Silence. She gnawed her lip, her hands clasped together in front of her.

'You won't be riding them?' she asked at last, lifting her eyes to his. He could tell how much the question cost her. There was satisfaction in making her wait, after the frustration she'd caused him.

'You would like to see me again?'

She blushed to the roots of her hair, her hands twisting together. She reacted like a virgin, confronting desire for the first time. But her eyes had already told him another story. She was more experienced than that. Still, the sight intrigued him. It really would be a pleasure, learning more about this woman.

'For the painting—if you wouldn't mind?'

Who could resist those wide eyes, the rosebud lips?

'I suppose I could ride here. If you really want me.'

The words pulsed in the silence between them. If she wanted him. He knew in the intense hush between them that she did, indeed, want him.

'How long would it take? The painting?' Better if she felt he was doing her a favour.

'A few days? Three, four mornings?' She couldn't conceal her excitement; it was there in her glittering eyes, the energy vibrating from every line in her body.

'Four mornings.' He paused. 'Very well. I will give you the mornings.' He couldn't prevent the smile that curled his lips. 'If you will give me the afternoons.'

# CHAPTER TWO

The afternoons? Rosalie blinked. Surely she was hearing things.

But, looking up into those lustrous eyes, she doubted it. The devil was there, lurking in the darkness and tempting her to do something stupid like say yes.

But yes to what?

It couldn't be what she thought. Could it?

'I'm sorry? What did you say?'

'I will give up my mornings until you have finished your painting if, in exchange, you spend the afternoons with me.'

Simple, his bland expression seemed to say, but his eyes told another story. Their brilliant glitter was too avid, almost hungry.

'I don't understand,' she said, edging away a fraction. Who was this man? Suddenly her sense of being crowded by him and his horses took on another, more sinister air. A chill shivered down Rosalie's spine as memories of the past she'd worked so hard to forget flooded back. The hairs on her arms rose and her mouth dried.

Her fear was intense, immediate and completely unstoppable.

His gaze bored into hers for a long moment, as if he knew what was going on in her mind. She saw his straight brows lift a fraction, his nostrils widen as if in surprise, and then the horses were moving away, parting to leave her standing alone. Without their warm bodies so close, the sea breeze seemed suddenly cool and she shivered.

'It's straightforward enough,' he said as he wheeled the mares round to face her. His voice dropped to a reassuring burr. She assumed it was reassurance she felt—that unfurling heat in her belly that welled and spread as he spoke. It couldn't be anything else.

'I'm recuperating from an injury and tired of my own company. Now I'm mobile again but under doctor's orders not to travel, while I do some physiotherapy and they check my recovery is complete.' He shrugged and the movement of those wide shoulders seemed unutterably weary, bored even. 'A few hours of company would take my mind off all the things I want to do but can't.'

Somehow she doubted he was a man who had to ask a stranger for companionship. Even now, her nerves still jangling from the adrenaline rush of tension, she felt the impact of his attraction. He radiated power and strength and something potently male. Something that made her aware of a small, hollow, yearning ache deep inside.

'I'm sure you have friends who—'

'But that's the problem,' he murmured. 'In my arrogance, my impatience to put all this behind me, I warned them off visiting until I was better.' His lips curled up in a rueful smile that made him look younger, more approachable. 'Call me proud, but I didn't want sympathy while I limped about.'

'Still, I don't think I—'

'I'm quite respectable,' he assured her. And the glint of strong white teeth in that beautiful aristocratic face told her he didn't usually have to vouch for his respectability. 'My name is Arik Kareem Ben Hassan. My home is here.' He gestured to the fortress hugging the cliff behind him.

Rosalie felt her eyes widen. He *lived* in that massive castle? Somehow she'd thought it must be a museum or national treasure or something. Not a house.

His easy assurance, his air of authority, and the way he handled those purebred horses, as if born to the saddle, made her suspect he wasn't a servant. And he spoke English so fluently he must have spent a lot of time overseas. So did he *own* the place?

'You can ask about me at your hotel if you wish. Everyone knows me—mention the Sheikh Ben Hassan.'

Rosalie's eyebrows shot up. A sheikh! Impossible that there could be two such stunning men, both with the same title, here in Q'aroum.

'But I thought the royal prince was the Sheikh.' Certainly that was how her brother-in-law was addressed, though to her he had always just been Rafiq, the gorgeous man who'd swept her sister, Belle, right off her feet.

The man before her shook his head. 'The prince is our head of state but each tribe has its own sheikh. My people live in the easternmost islands of Q'aroum and I am their leader.'

He sent her a dazzling smile that made her insides roll over. 'Don't worry.' Even from here she could see the mischief dancing in his eyes. 'Contrary to popular fiction, and despite the temptation, we do not make a habit of kidnapping beautiful blonde strangers for our harems. Not any more.'

Rosalie opened her mouth to ask if that had ever, really, been the custom, then realised she already knew the answer. This island nation was rife with exotic tales of plunder and piracy. Its famed wealth had grown centuries ago from rapacious attacks on passing ships. The Q'aroumis had long ago earned a reputation as fierce warriors who conversely had an appreciation of not only wealth but beauty. As a result their booty had, if legend were to be believed, included beautiful women as well as riches.

'But you have me at a disadvantage,' he continued. 'I don't even know your name.'

'It's Rosalie. Rosalie Winters.' She felt gauche standing here, hands clasped together as she lifted her chin to look up at the superb man controlling those fidgety horses with such lazy, yet ruthless grace.

Of course he had no ulterior motive in wanting her company. A man with his looks and, no doubt, wealth, wouldn't be interested in a very ordinary Australian tourist. He was bored, that was all, and no doubt intrigued to find someone on his beach.

'It's a pleasure to meet you, Rosalie.' His voice was deep and smooth, rippling across her skin and warming her deep inside. 'You must call me Arik.'

'Thank you.' She inclined her head and stretched her lips into a tense smile, panicked by the thrill of pleasure coursing through her, the impact of his smooth velvety voice.

'I look forward to our afternoons together,' he said and Rosalie's breath caught as his smile disappeared and his hooded eyelids lowered just a fraction. Her instant impression was of brooding, waiting sensuality. It should repel her—she knew it should—but somehow this man's casually harnessed male power and potent sexuality intrigued her.

She shook her head. Impossible. She'd learned her lesson well. Men and their desires were never to be trusted. She'd come to her senses as soon as he left.

'I'm sorry but—'

'You do not wish to spend time with me?' He sounded astonished, as if he'd never before encountered a refusal. His eyebrows rose in disbelief.

It would do him good to realise he couldn't smooth talk every woman he met.

'Thank you for the offer,' she said, conscious of the need not to offend, 'but I wouldn't feel comfortable alone with a man I didn't know.' That much was the truth. No need to explain that it was his potent maleness, combined with the gleam of appreciation she'd recognised in his eyes, that guaranteed she could never let herself trust him.

His brows levelled as he stared at her. His scrutiny was so intense she could swear it burned across her skin, invoking an embarrassed blush up her throat. She felt vulnerable, as if he saw too much of her fears and insecurities, as if his scrutiny stripped away layer upon layer of the self-protective armour she'd forged for herself.

'You have my word, Rosalie, that I would never force my attentions where they were not wanted.' He drew himself straighter on his mount, every line of his lean, powerful body and every muscle in his face rigid with outraged pride. His strong hands, so relaxed a moment ago, clenched hard on the reins and his horse danced sideways, rolling its eyes as if it sensed its master's displeasure.

Despite herself, Rosalie felt her blush intensify to a burning vivid crimson, flooding up and over her cheeks. But she stood her ground and met his haughty stare.

'I appreciate your assurance,' she said, consciously avoiding the use of his name and the intimacy that implied. 'And I apologise if I've offended you, but—'

'But you are right to be cautious with men you do not know.' He nodded and some of the tension left his face. His lips curved in a rueful smile. Once again she felt that throb of awareness between them. Unwanted but only too real.

What was happening to her? He was a chance-met stranger. Despite his good looks and his sex appeal, he should mean nothing to her.

'I do not wish to make you uncomfortable, but I have to admit I would appreciate your company. I'm obviously a bad patient, not cut out for solitude and quiet recovery.' Again that shrug of wide shoulders. 'We could perhaps visit some of the local sights, if that would ease your mind. There are always plenty of people about in the marketplace and the old city. We need not be alone.'

Now she really did feel awkward, as if she'd overreacted to the most innocent of requests.

'And,' he added with slow deliberation, 'the pleasure of your presence would count as suitable recompense for my assistance to your art.'

The sting in the tail, Rosalie realised, watching his shrewd eyes narrow assessingly.

She hesitated, bent and picked up her bulging canvas bag to give herself time to collect her thoughts. This man made her nervous, her damp palms and roiling stomach were testament to that. Yet the trembling sensation still tingling down her backbone in response to his last smile was proof of something more dangerous. Interest, awareness, excitement. That was what really worried her. The fear of the unknown.

On the other hand, there was her painting. The thrill of creative energy she'd experienced this morning was addictive, intoxicating. It promised something wonderful. She'd give almost anything to be able to work again. Maybe this painting would be the key she needed to resume her art. A key that she'd thought gone for ever. How could she pass that up? It could be her last chance to regain something of what she'd lost.

She drew a slow breath and met his eyes. 'Thank you. I'd appreciate seeing more of the island with someone who knows it so well.'

Simple, easy—she hadn't committed to anything dangerous. So why did she feel as if she'd just taken a step into the fraught unknown?

His smile was a blinding flash that stalled her breath in her throat.

'Thank you, Rosalie.' Her name on his lips sounded different: exotic and intriguing. 'And I promise that I will never do anything that you do not like. You have only to say the word if you object to something.'

Rosalie stared up at his satisfied expression, his relaxed pose, and wondered if she'd done the right thing. He looked too…smug, as if he'd got more out of the bargain than she suspected.

That had to be her perennially suspicious mind. She'd conditioned herself to be wary. Now she'd forgotten how to take people at face value. Perhaps this was her chance to rectify the balance, relax a little on her holiday and learn not to freeze up when she was with a man.

'Thank you…Arik. I'll look forward to seeing you tomorrow morning.'

Arik watched her turn and walk away, barefoot along the damp sand.

The sound of her soft voice saying his name, the sight of her lush mouth forming the word, had pulled the muscles tight in his belly. He felt a gnawing ache there, a greedy hunger that had grown in intensity once he'd come close enough to see her properly.

From a distance Rosalie Winters had been desirable, tempting and intriguing. Close up she was stunning.

Her eyes were wide and surprisingly innocent, more alluring than those of most women he met, with their consciously seductive glances that invited flirtation. Her skin looked soft as a petal, making him eager to experience it for himself. Her heart-shaped face, her perfect pink bow of a mouth and her rose gold hair, like gilt with the hint of a blush, were all superb.

Yet there was something else at the core of her attractiveness. Not her air of vulnerability—that had been a surprise and it had evoked in him a sudden surge of protectiveness so strong he'd wondered if he should shelve his plan completely. Turn around and leave her.

But he wasn't into self-denial.

Maybe it was the fact that she hadn't immediately tried to pursue *him*. He'd had women chasing after him since he'd reached puberty. He had to do no more than indicate his interest to have whatever woman he wanted. Even the discovery that he was a sheikh, a leader of his people, had failed to arouse anything more than mild curiosity in her. That news had, in the past, led to some women becoming almost embarrassingly fascinated. They were so busy fantasising about his sex life they had no concept of his real life: his responsibilities and his manic work schedule.

Not that he objected to the right woman taking an interest in his sex life.

At the moment Rosalie Winters was the right woman.

She was a new phenomenon: gorgeous, naturally seductive, but with no apparent awareness of her own devastating sex appeal. That air of innocence was incredibly alluring, even to a man who'd never been interested in deflowering virgins. For a moment he'd almost believed she'd never been with a man—till he read the knowledge, the wariness in her eyes. They told him she'd known at least one man far too well and had been disillusioned by the experience. Her caution had even, for an instant, verged on fear. And, with that realisation, searing pain had stabbed through him.

Who was she? How had she got under his skin so completely? And why did he feel that seducing her would be an unforgettable experience?

Arik was determined to uncover her secrets, would delight in discovering what went on in her mind almost as much as he'd enjoy possessing her sleek, ripe body.

She was a challenge unlike any he'd met. Already his blood ran hot in expectation of gratification to come. He would make her burn for him too, sigh out her desire for him, her need for fulfilment that only he could provide.

He watched her disappear round the rocks at the end of the beach. Not once had she glanced back. As if she'd known he sat here, watching her, anticipating tomorrow with barely concealed impatience.

He thought of his promise to her: not to do anything she didn't like. He grinned. Of course she'd enjoy what he had in mind. He was no untried youth, nor a selfish hedonist seeking nothing but his own release. He was a man who fully appreciated the pleasure a woman's satisfaction could bring. Whose lovers never had complaints about his ability to arouse and satisfy.

No, despite her caution, he was sure Rosalie Winters would never say the word that would prevent them both enjoying the ultimate pleasure together.

Rosalie paused at the headland. It marked the end of all that was safe. The point of no return. Far behind her lay the town, still slumbering in the dawn light.

Ahead lay the private cove with its ancient fort, and danger. She felt it in her bones. But what sort of danger? Yesterday she'd surely overreacted, overwhelmed by her excitement to be painting again and by her response to *him*.

She drew a deep breath. Did she really want to do this? All yesterday afternoon, while she was busy with Amy, her thoughts had returned to the man she'd met beyond this next headland: Arik Ben Hassan, and his invitation. He was a man unlike any she'd ever met.

Unbidden, a curl of excitement twisted low in her belly. The same sensation that had teased her all yesterday, reminding her that, despite the way she chose to live her life, and the needs she'd so long suppressed, she was, above all, a woman. With a woman's weakness for a man who epitomised male power, strength and beauty.

That had to explain her restless night. The disturbing dreams that had her tossing in her sleep. She'd awoken time and again to find her heart pounding and her temperature soaring.

The first time she'd put it down to stress. Her mother and Amy had left for the capital that afternoon to stay with Rosalie's sister, Belle, and her family. Originally Rosalie had planned to go too. She'd never spent the night away from Amy, not since her daughter was born, and the wrench had been just as hard as she'd expected. Not that Amy had been fazed—she'd been too busy looking forward to visiting the palace again and seeing her baby cousin.

It was Rosalie's mum who'd convinced her to stay. Maggie Winters had been thrilled to discover her daughter had taken her art supplies out during the early hours while Amy slept. She'd insisted Rosalie stay on for a few more days in the house Rafiq had arranged. The time alone would do her good, she'd insisted. Rosalie had never had a break from the demands of single parenthood. She needed time to herself and it would be good for Amy too, experiencing something different for a few days.

Her mother had been so insistent, but more, so upset when she'd planned to leave the island, Rosalie hadn't had the heart to persist. After all, she owed her mum so much. She was her rock.

Rosalie shuddered, recalling that day over three years ago when she'd stumbled from a taxi into her mother's outstretched arms. She'd been falling apart, shaking and nauseous, barely coherent in the aftermath of shock, but her mum had taken it all in her stride, not even pressing for details till Rosalie was ready to talk. And then it had spilled out—the Friday night date, the crowded party, the spiked drink and Rosalie waking in a strange bed to the realisation she'd been assaulted. Raped.

Even now the memory made her feel ill.

She knew it was her mum's loving support that had given

her the courage to put the past behind her and create a new life for herself. Especially since her new life included Amy, legacy of that disastrous night.

Yet, despite the progress she'd made, the wonderful fulfilment of motherhood and her determination not to look back, she knew her mum secretly fretted over her.

Was it any wonder Rosalie hadn't admitted that her attempts to rekindle her artistic skills were an abysmal failure?

Until yesterday, that was. It had all come together then, the sure light touch that had been her trademark in the days when she'd dreamed of making a name for herself as an artist.

Even then she'd been tempted to turn her back on what could be a false promise. Far safer to travel with her family to Q'aroum's capital than take a chance on the unknown. Who knew whether she really *could* paint?

And was she up to dealing with a man like Arik Ben Hassan? A man who probably had the world at his feet and who on a whim had decided he wanted her company. Given her background, she was the last person to keep him amused with casual small talk and witty observations, if that was what he expected.

He hadn't a clue about her. And that was the way she preferred it. Especially since he'd invaded her thoughts, even her dreams, in the twenty-four hours since she'd met him. He was dangerous to her peace of mind. To the delicate balance of her life.

But he was the key to her art. At least for now, until she worked out whether yesterday had been a fluke or a new start.

She hitched her bag higher on her shoulder and made herself walk on.

He came to her like a prince out of a fairy tale—strong, silent and commanding. The epitome of maidenly longings, Rosalie decided, trying to make herself smile to unwind the tension coiling tight in her chest.

It didn't work.

The sight of him: tall and devastatingly attractive, this time in lightweight beige trousers and another white shirt, weakened her knees. Closer he came, the muffled thud of hooves a vibration on the sand more than a sound. The wind caught his shirt and dragged it back, outlining the lean strength of his torso and wide, straight shoulders. The gleam of dawn gilded his face, throwing one side into deep shadow that accentuated the remarkable angles of his face, drawing the eye to those stunning cheekbones and the severe angle of his jaw.

Rosalie swallowed hard, then reached for the water she'd brought. She was parched, her mouth dried by the sight of him and by the sudden longing she experienced. A yearning that was strange and new and appalling.

This was a mistake. A disastrous mistake. But it was too late to leave. He'd seen her the moment he'd ridden down on to the beach. And she had too much pride to turn tail now and leave him wondering why she was scared of him. Especially when she didn't know the answer to that herself.

'*Saba'a alkair*, Rosalie.' His face was gravely courteous as he inclined his head, his voice the deeply seductive tone she remembered from her dream. She shivered.

'*Saba'a alkair*.'

'Your pronunciation is excellent.'

'Thank you.' No need to tell him she'd learned her few words of Arabic from her brother-in-law, another local and a man of immense patience with her faltering efforts.

'You slept well?' His scrutiny was intense, sweeping over her like a touch, so the blood heated beneath her skin.

'Thank you, I did,' she lied. 'Only one horse today?' She was eager to change the subject.

He shrugged, drawing her attention once more to the spare power of his torso. She wished she could look away.

'I thought one would be enough for your purposes. But if you want—'

'No, no. That's fine.' It was the magic between rider and mount that she wanted to capture. She turned away, as if to busy herself with her gear, but a sudden movement made her turn back. It was him, Arik, swinging his leg over the horse and dismounting.

'What are you doing?' The words were out before she could stop them. She heard her squeak of horror echo even now as the silence reverberated between them.

His eyebrows tilted up as he looped the reins in his hand. 'I thought that was obvious,' he said and took a single long step closer.

Rosalie had thought him impressive on horseback, imposing enough to dominate any scene. But that was before he stood close to her, enveloping her with his air of restrained power. She felt his heat, detected again his spicy natural scent, and more. As she angled her chin up to meet his eyes, she experienced something else, something primal and powerful, a spell that kept her rooted to the spot. She watched him with widening eyes as her pulse thudded a quickening tattoo.

This close she could see his skin gleamed with health, his mouth was slightly crooked; when he smiled it curved up more on the left. And his eyes—she couldn't believe it! Even from less than a metre away, they were black as night, gleaming with humour as she struggled to find her composure.

'It's traditional here to seal a bargain with a gesture of trust,' he murmured, 'and our agreement is important to me.'

The flutter of panic in her stomach transformed into an earth tremor of mixed horror and anticipation as he leaned closer. He couldn't mean to—

Strong fingers closed around her right hand, she felt the scrape of calluses as he cradled it in his, then he firmed his grip.

'We always shake hands on a deal here, Rosalie.' His words were low, soft, making her lean even closer to hear.

His gaze, dark and unfathomable, held hers and she felt a sensation of weightlessness. For a long moment the illusion held as she stood, enthralled by the heat and promise in his eyes.

Then common sense reasserted itself. She straightened her spine. 'Of course.' She nodded, hoping to seem businesslike. Just a handshake. She could cope with that.

But, even as she reassured herself, he lifted her hand in his, held it just below his lips so she felt the rhythm of his breath hot on her skin. She blinked.

'But with a lady, a handshake is not enough.'

Was that glitter in his gaze laughter or something else?

No, it wasn't laughter. She just had time to realise it was something more dangerous when his mouth brushed her skin. The kiss was warm, soft and seductive. Her breath hitched as their gazes locked. His eyes were pure black. Black as night, dark as desire. Inviting, beckoning. A blaze of flame licked through her abdomen, igniting a flare that grew and spread like fire in her bloodstream.

She shuddered as his lips caressed her skin, pressing more firmly and somehow, impossibly, finding an erogenous zone on the back of her hand. Her chest heaved as she gasped for oxygen. He paused so long that she felt warm air feather across her skin as he exhaled once, twice, three times.

At last he lifted his head, but the stark hunger in his face made her want to turn tail and run back the way she'd come.

# CHAPTER THREE

Now he knew. Her skin tasted sweetly addictive, its texture as smooth as cream against his lips. He wanted to bend his head again and lick her hand, turn it over and lave her palm, drawing her flavour, rich as wild honey, into his mouth.

He wanted to set his tongue against the frenetic pulse he felt fluttering at her delicate wrist, kiss her arm, her sensitive inner elbow, take his time in working his way to her collarbone, her throat, awash now with a tide of rose-pink. Then her lips.

His hand tightened around hers as his gaze dropped to her mouth, a perfect Cupid's bow of feminine invitation. Her lips parted just a fraction, as if in unconscious invitation, and the storm of longing notched up inside him.

*Never* had he experienced need so instantaneous, obliterating all else. It was like a roaring, racing conflagration swirling almost out of control.

And all he'd done was kiss her hand! Even the scent of her, like the perfume of dew on rosebuds, was enough to test his self-possession.

His heart pounded against his ribs, adrenaline surged in his bloodstream, inciting action. His every sense clamoured for fulfilment. Here. Now. On the hard-packed sand where the sun's early rays would light her body to gold and amber for his delectation.

He snagged one rough breath. Watched her eyes widen and realised his grip had firmed too much. Another breath and he loosened his hold, still unwilling to relinquish her hand.

But she tugged it away, slipped her fingers from his and cradled them with her other hand between her breasts. The unthinking gesture pulled the soft cotton of her shirt tight and his breath seized in his lungs as he eyed the outline of her bra.

'A handshake would have done,' she whispered, her voice shaky.

Arik almost laughed at the absurdity of it. She was chastising him for being too forward in kissing her hand. How would she react if she knew he was hard with need for her? That just the sight of her plain bra beneath that prudish high-buttoned shirt and the taste of her against his lips made him hot with desire?

But his laughter fled as he looked in her eyes and saw the confusion there. Confusion and…trepidation?

She was scared of him, his golden girl?

Instantly he took a half pace backwards, watching the way her dilated eyes seemed to focus somewhere near his chin as her breathing slowly evened out.

She looked as if no man had ever kissed her hand. More, as if the dance of desire between the sexes was something new to her.

Impossible. Surely in Australia men were men enough to pursue a beauty as delicate and enticing as this one. It still amazed him that she was alone, no male hovering close to guard against intruders.

'I see our customs are different to what you are used to. I meant no offence.'

He wondered if she'd be satisfied with that explanation. Surely even an innocent would realise that a formal kiss on the fingers was completely different from the sensuous introduction they'd just experienced. Or maybe she'd ignore the fact, pretend it hadn't happened.

She nodded, turned her head away to stare at the glow of light on the horizon. 'Of course. I understand.'

He was right—she was avoiding the truth.

But he'd achieved his aim. She was *aware* of him now. Not just as a distant figure on horseback to be captured in paints, but as a man. Flesh and blood. Her agitated breathing, the quick sidelong glance at him, the way she bit down on the corner of her mouth, all affirmed it.

The first step towards his goal. He smothered a smile and turned towards Layla, saddled this time so he could mount more easily with his stiff leg.

'Where do you want me?'

The question caught Rosalie by surprise and her mouth rounded in an O of shock. Faint colour warmed her cheeks and Arik held his mouth tight so as not to betray his satisfied grin. So, it had been more than just an introduction for her too. That was a guilty expression if ever he'd seen one. Obviously she *did* want him.

Now it was just a matter of getting her to admit it.

Rosalie put her hand to her back and stretched out the stiffness there. She'd sat too long, absorbed in her work, and now her muscles protested.

She looked at the canvas before her and fought down bubbling excitement. It was too early to tell. Far too early to know if this would be anything worthwhile. *But*, a tiny part of her wanted to crow, it was promising. Definitely promising. Certainly far better than her faltering attempts earlier in the week.

After her tension when she'd begun this morning, she thought she'd never be able to settle down and work. She'd been strung taut like a bow, wary of the knowing light in Arik's eyes, the flagrant desire she read in his face, and scared to betray the secret answering yearning that spiralled deep inside her.

That had taken her completely by surprise, even after yesterday's encounter and last night's restless dreams. She'd experienced nothing like it. Even in the days when she had been young and innocent. Her teenage fantasies had been about romance and happy endings. They'd never been raw with the force of untrammelled physical desire.

It had been like a surge of white-hot electricity, the arousal she'd felt as Arik had taken her hand in his, moved his lips against her skin and made her want…him. The jolt of energy had arced deep inside her, straight to her womb where the aching emptiness had been like a throbbing pain.

No one had said it would ever be like that.

'You're happy with what you've done?' She looked up to find him leaning towards her from the back of his horse. There was a safe distance between them now but it wasn't enough. Rosalie suspected that with this man there would never be enough distance for her to feel secure.

'It's not bad,' she said cautiously, turning away from his regard.

He saw too much, she knew that already. Though not, she hoped, nearly as much as she wanted to hide from him.

'And so we're finishing for the morning?' The question was straightforward, but it held a note of something unsettling.

'Yes.' She nodded. 'All finished for now.'

'Good.' He nudged his horse away and dragged something from his pocket—a cellphone. As Rosalie started tidying up her supplies she heard his voice, low and warm, as he spoke in his native tongue. She loved the lilt of it, the fluidity, and her hands slowed as she listened.

She remembered the teasing sound of his voice yesterday, as he'd chivvied the horses. A thrill skittered down her spine as she imagined him speaking, his tone intimately caressing, pitched for her alone.

Appalled at herself, she began to shove her gear away with

more force than prudence. She couldn't believe her wayward imagination. *Never* had she fantasised about a man in this way. She shook her head, wondering what had changed. This instant overwhelming attraction was terrifying. It was the sort of attraction that she guessed led to one-night stands.

For an instant the horrible irony of that thought struck her, but she shoved it aside. She had no time for self-pity. The past was gone.

But that still left her way out of her depth.

Five minutes later she was packed, all except her easel and canvas, when the rumble of an engine made her look up. It was a four-wheel drive approaching over a stony track from the ridge above. Arik was already riding to meet it.

As she watched, a couple of men got out and, following his instructions, began unloading something from the back of the vehicle. Soon it began to take shape, high on the beach, as a large canvas awning. No, a tent, with one side open, facing the sea.

Arik walked towards her, his naturally long stride shortening almost imperceptibly on each second step. His damaged leg. The realisation brought a crazy rush of sympathy for whatever pain he'd suffered.

Rosalie shook her head. What had got into her? She'd known the man a little more than a day, if she could be said to *know* him.

'If you permit, I'll have your work taken to my home and brought along tomorrow morning at first light. That way you won't have to carry it each day.' He paused, then added, 'I will personally vouch that it will be handled appropriately. My mother is an amateur artist and my staff understand that it is more than their lives are worth to damage a work in progress.' His smile was charming, robbing his words of any threat.

'I…of course. That's very thoughtful of you.' Pointless to assert that she didn't want it leaving her hands. That she'd feel safer with the canvas in her own keeping. Was she superstitious enough to fear that without it in her possession she might lose this second chance?

Reluctantly she nodded and followed him to the vehicle, where he'd tethered his mare. She clutched her tote bag close as he stowed first the portable easel and then her canvas in the rear of the four-wheel drive.

The men had finished setting up the tent and nodded as Arik spoke again to them in their own language. Then one of them turned and said with a bow, 'I will look after your painting, miss. It will be safe with me.'

She only had time to smile and nod her thanks before they were on their way, one in the four-wheel drive and the other leading the mare up the track, leaving Rosalie alone with Arik.

Her heart thumped an uncomfortable rhythm and she told herself not to be stupid. She'd been alone with him for hours. But somehow this was different. No easel to hide behind. No horse to demand his attention.

Silently she followed him to the tent. It was far too large for a beach shelter—a dozen people could easily have stood inside it.

But then this was far more than a shelter from the sun, she discovered as she rounded one side and found herself looking in. It was—luxury. A jumble of rich colours and fabrics, from the patterned floor coverings to the sumptuous pile of cushions heaped on the floor. A low folding table with a round brass top gleamed in the centre of the space and on it, incongruously, sat a huge vacuum flask. A cool chest stood beside it, making Rosalie wonder suddenly if there was any food in it. She'd been working solidly for hours and now she was starving.

'You would like some refreshment?' Arik's deep voice said beside her.

'Yes, thank you.' She avoided his eyes and watched as he bent to collect something from just inside the tent. A copper ewer, soap and a linen towel which he folded over his arm.

'Here.' He held out the soap to her. She took it and held out her hands while he poured a steady stream of warm water over them. She inhaled the fragrance of sandalwood as she lathered and washed, then handed him the soap and rinsed her hands.

Rosalie reached for the finely woven towel, trying not to touch his arm. There was something too intimate about the situation, for all he stood as still and unthreatening as a statue. The warm soapy scent rose between them, but this close to him she recognised his own unique fragrance: male skin and just a hint of sea salt and horse.

She breathed in deeply and held out her hand for the ewer. 'Let me.'

She kept her eyes down, away from his. Instead she found herself watching his strong, well-shaped hands as he soaped them, sliding one against the other slowly and thoroughly. Rosalie stared.

She'd drawn countless hands over the years. Had sketched them relaxed, fisted, holding various objects. Just as she'd sketched naked models with never a flicker of emotion.

But standing here, watching those long powerful hands slide together, seeing the corded muscles and sinews of his forearms where he'd rolled back his sleeves, Rosalie found herself swallowing hard as excitement stirred deep inside her.

He put down the soap and she tipped more water over his hands, his wrists, wishing she could reach out and trace their tensile strength for herself.

He reached for the towel she'd draped over her arm, barely brushing her shirt with his fingers. She almost sighed with relief when she could step away, put a precious pace or two between them.

'Thank you, Rosalie.' His voice broke the silence between them and she darted a look up at him. His eyes were unreadable, the obsidian-black that she still couldn't believe. She wished she could read his thoughts. Then, as his nostrils widened a fraction, his mouth curled up in a half smile, she was suddenly glad she couldn't. No doubt she was totally transparent in the way she reacted to his sheer maleness. But she couldn't help herself.

That was what scared her most. Her reaction to this man.

'Do you usually picnic in such style?' She tried not to sound too impressed and the words came out accusing.

He shrugged and motioned for her to enter. 'If I'm entertaining I prefer that my guests are comfortable and well taken care of.'

Rosalie just bet he did a lot of entertaining. Especially of women.

She hesitated, aware once more of how isolated they were. There had been no one else on the beach all morning. And in the tent they'd be out of sight even from the windows of the fortress on the hill. She eyed the tumble of cushions on the floor and wondered what he had in mind for their afternoon together.

'Ahmed will be back in an hour to clear away the remains of our meal,' Arik said from beside her. 'Then I thought we might drive into the town and do some sightseeing.'

'That sounds lovely, thank you.'

*See, it's just company he wants. Someone to talk to. You've grown too suspicious.*

Nevertheless, she felt uneasily as if she'd committed herself to far more than lunch as she slipped off her shoes and stepped into the tent. The soft fabric beneath her feet was sheer decadence. The colours, the textures, even the scent was exotic, like something out of an Arabian fantasy. Just like the man at her side: the epitome of absolute male strength and sensuality. It was all too easy to picture him in flowing robes with a scimitar in his hands. Or in a bed with silken sheets where some dusky beauty kept him occupied.

'Please.' He gestured towards the pile of cushions. 'Make yourself comfortable.'

Gingerly she moved forward, averting her flushed face. She settled herself on a large cushion, resisting the temptation to flop back and let her tired body relax on the luxurious pile. Nevertheless, she felt some of the stiffness seep out of her as she tucked her legs into a comfortable position and looked out at the fabulous coastal scene before her.

Beside her, but not too close, Arik settled with a single easy movement of graceful power. He didn't crowd her and her breathing eased a little. But then, she supposed it wasn't his style to crowd a woman. She was sure that with his looks and obvious wealth he was usually fending them off instead. He'd have no need to do anything but smile and women would flock to him.

Surely she'd mistaken his intense expression earlier. She'd read raw hunger in his face but maybe she'd been wrong. Perhaps she'd just assumed that was what he felt—a mirror of her own sudden longing. She'd been so overcome by the stifling sensation of heat when he'd kissed her hand that she hadn't been able to think straight.

After all, why would he be interested in someone as ordinary as her? She wasn't glamorous or chic. She was a working mum. How much more mundane could you get?

'Coffee?'

'Thank you.' The scent of it as he opened the flask was heavenly, reminding her that she'd been too nervous this morning to have more than a glass of water and a piece of toast before she left the house. She watched him pour the hot coffee and decided it was better to concentrate on her surroundings than on her growing fascination with those magnificent hands.

'This—' she gestured to the interior of the tent '—is amazing.' Only now did she notice the tiny side table with its bowl of full velvety roses. She'd assumed the scent was some sort of rose essence sprinkled on the gorgeous cushions.

'Not too over-the-top for you?' One eyebrow tilted and

there was a gleam of humour in his dark eyes as he handed her a cup of coffee and gestured towards milk and sugar on the table before her.

She shook her head, permitting herself a tiny answering smile. 'It's more luxurious than what we have back home.' Which was a towel and maybe an old beach umbrella for shade. 'But it's lovely. And the coffee's wonderful. Thank you.' She sighed as the rich liquid slid down her throat.

Arik watched her eyes close for a moment as she savoured the coffee.

Even with a tiny smudge of paint high on her cheek, her cotton shirt creased and her long hair slipping from the ponytail that secured it, she was temptation personified. That creamy-soft skin, a pale gold that showed each delicate blush, and those eyes, hauntingly erotic. The sensual curves designed for a man's pleasure. And her long ripple of hair the colour of a dawn sunburst. All too easily he could visualise those strands spread across the pillows behind her as she lay beneath him, an invitation to his touch.

He itched for her. Burned for her.

But she wasn't ready. She wasn't like his usual women: eager and flirty, sometimes too eager.

Rosalie Winters was different. She was ripe for him, he'd easily read her body's unconscious signals. But her mind was another matter. This was a woman who did not give herself lightly.

Yet he knew instinctively she'd be worth waiting for. This time it wouldn't be about almost instant gratification. For once he was willing to delay. With Rosalie he was discovering that anticipation was part of the pleasure.

'So where is home? What part of Australia?'

'Queensland. In the north east.'

'I know it, or part of it. I've dived on the Great Barrier Reef.'

Her eyes widened. What had she expected? That he'd never left his island home?

'That's where I come from. A small town on the coast just north of Cairns.'

'You're blessed with beautiful country.'

She looked out across the bay. 'And so are you.'

'Thank you.' Despite the fact that he spent most of his time elsewhere, Q'aroum was his home. Her simple compliment pleased him.

'And have you always lived near Cairns?'

She shook her head and he saw the rose-gold strands of hair snag on her shirt. 'I lived in Brisbane once.'

'For work?' Her reticence intrigued him. He was accustomed to women demanding his attention, vying for his interest.

'I was only there for a year. To attend art school.' She kept her gaze fixed on the sea but he saw the way her mouth tightened, her lips pulling flat.

Not a good experience, then. He wondered what had happened. His curiosity about her grew with every passing hour.

'You didn't like the city life?'

She shrugged, leaving her shoulders hunched and defensive. 'It didn't work out.'

There was a wealth of pain in her voice and he decided against prying. But he'd give a great deal to know what had caused her such hurt. A man, he supposed. Only a failed relationship could cause such pain, or so his friends told him. He'd never had any such problems.

'And now you live on the coast and work as an artist.'

She shot him a glance he couldn't decipher and shook her head once more. 'I work part-time in a child care centre. I decided against art as a career.'

'I understand it's a very difficult field in which to make a living. But with your talent that must have been a difficult decision.' Obviously she loved her art. She'd been so totally absorbed in it this morning that he'd been piqued at how little attention she'd paid him—as anything more than a necessary part of the scene. It was as if nothing else had existed for her.

She laughed, a short, hard sound that held no humour, dragging at something deep inside him.

'I didn't have much choice in the matter.'

Another look at her face and he decided against pursuing the issue, for now.

'And you like working with children?'

Her face softened. She was so easy to read, and yet she was still an enigma. 'I love it. Working with little ones puts your life in perspective.'

'I can see you're looking forward to becoming a mother yourself one day.'

She turned and snared him with those smoky-green eyes. Her mouth widened into a smile that lit her face. 'I'm already a mother. My little girl, Amy, is two and a half.'

Arik felt his stare harden as her words sank in, something, some strong emotion, balled in his gut, drawing each muscle taut to the point of pain.

He turned away to refill his cup, desperately gathering his control about him.

Fury, that was what it was.

His frown turned to a scowl as he recognised the emotion, hard as a knot, inside him. Anger. And jealousy.

The idea that she'd carried another man's child, had *belonged* so intimately to another, burned deep, eating like acid.

The intensity of sensation shocked him. Shook him out of his complacent belief in himself as an easygoing man. There was nothing easygoing about the churning turmoil in the pit of his stomach. It was a surge of pure old-fashioned covetousness. Envy that some other man had enjoyed what he so wanted.

Arik couldn't believe it. He'd never been jealous in his life!

'My congratulations,' he murmured, trying to concentrate on pouring the coffee. 'Does she look like you or like her father?'

So absorbed was he in mastering the roiling mass of his jealousy that he almost missed her hesitation.

'Everyone says she looks like me.'

He turned back and offered her the flask of coffee, but she shook her head.

'She must be a very pretty little girl, then.' Even that was enough to heighten the glow in Rosalie's cheeks. As if she wasn't used to receiving such compliments.

Were Australian men so clumsy, then? Or, the thought suddenly emerged, had she been avoiding them? Had she been burned by the relationship with her daughter's father so that she shied away from men?

That was a definite possibility, given her skittishness. Arik filed away the thought for later consideration. 'Your daughter isn't with you?'

Rosalie shook her head. 'My mother's looking after her this week. I'm by myself for now.'

Arik worked hard to keep the satisfaction from his face. Alone for the week. And perhaps a little lonely? Perfect.


Rosalie watched as he unpacked their lunch from the cool-box. It was a relief when he'd ceased his questions and begun to explain the dishes his cook had prepared. Not that he'd probed. Yet with him she felt defensive, as if she didn't trust him not to use the information against her.

*Ridiculous!* How could he? She hadn't said anything particularly personal. Just the bare bones of her life. And yet…she'd sensed a purpose behind his questions, as if he weren't just making small talk.

Arik Ben Hassan was too unsettling for her peace of mind.

Was that why she hadn't come clean about exactly who she was? The sister-in-law of the sovereign prince of Q'aroum.

She'd automatically shied away from the fact, eager to preserve her anonymity. Everywhere she and her mother went in Q'aroum, they'd been treated with such formal courtesy once people discovered their connection to the ruling family. It was nice to be just plain Rosalie Winters again.

Even now it seemed bizarre, her sister marrying into royalty. But it had taken just an hour spent with Rafiq, on his first visit to Australia, for her to understand why Belle had fallen for him.

Strong, protective, handsome and, above all, completely besotted with his new wife. The sort of man Rosalie could have fallen in love with herself.

The sort of man who was as rare as gold at the end of the rainbow.

She shot a sideways glance at her host, cataloguing the noble profile, the lean strength and easy grace of his actions.

Another stunningly attractive man. Yet, she sensed, a completely different personality to her brother-in-law. She couldn't imagine Arik settling down with just one woman. Those heavy-lidded eyes with their knowing, teasing gleam indicated he enjoyed the good life too much. No doubt he had the money and free time to indulge any whim. Why should he take life seriously?

She watched him unpack the platters and bowls of tempting local dishes—salads, dips, sesame bread and cold meats. All perfect. All exquisitely presented. Even for a man with his own private chef, surely this was no ordinary picnic?

'Arik?' His name sounded too good on her lips. She wished she hadn't used it. Especially when he turned round to her, that tempting half-smile tugging at his lips and changing his face from imposing to sexy.

'What is all this?' Her gesture encompassed the luxurious setting as well as the feast spread before her.

'A picnic lunch?' There was a twinkle in those dark eyes that almost made her smile, despite her wariness.

She shook her head. 'No, it's more than that.' She hesitated, wondering how big a fool she was about to make of herself. But she had to know. 'Please. I'm not into games. Exactly what is it you want from me?'

The humour faded from his eyes in an instant, replaced by a brooding severity she hadn't seen before. It caught her by surprise.

So did his hand, reaching out and enfolding hers. His touch was light but firm, his flesh warm and enticing. She sucked in a breath.

'Exactly?' His thumb stroked over hers, sending a shiver of excitement straight to her secret feminine core. 'I would like to know you better, Rosalie. *Much better.*' Another stroke of his thumb made her tremble.

'I want to become your lover.'

# CHAPTER FOUR

Rosalie wrenched her hand away. Dismay lit her face.

And something else. A dazzling instant of connection that told Arik he was right. She too felt the surge of desire between them. She wanted him and it scared her. He read vulnerability in her eyes, in the twist of her lips.

'No!' Her eyes boggled. 'I mean—'

'You're not interested in a short romance?'

She shook her head and long strands of rose gilt swirled around her neck. 'No. No, I'm not.'

His eyes narrowed as he took in her clenched fists, the rapid rise and fall of her breasts, her stormy eyes.

If he were a sensitive soul his ego might have been bruised by her vehemence. Instead he saw beyond her rejection to the inner pain she couldn't conceal. There was *something* there. Some deep-seated fear that made her deny him, and herself, the pleasure they would find together.

For an instant, impatience, pique at the unprecedented rejection, threatened to swamp him. Then sense reasserted itself. Much as she denied it, Rosalie was ripe for him. She couldn't conceal her body's eagerness. Or the way her eyes devoured him when she thought he wasn't aware.

He'd need time to thaw her shell of ice. But then, didn't he have time on his hands? She was a delectable challenge, yet with patience he'd triumph over her caution. He knew it. And victory would taste like paradise.

The certainty of her surrender added piquancy to the situation. Maybe he was jaded by easy conquests. The knowledge that he'd need his wits as well as charm to seduce her merely fired his determination to have her.

He would play a waiting game. *For now.*

'I apologise for embarrassing you, Rosalie.' Her eyes were huge in her face. 'Forgive me.'

She swallowed down hard. He watched the convulsive movement of her throat and tried not to wonder how soft her skin would be there. How tender the spot under the corner of her jaw, and further up her neck, just below her ear.

'That's it?' Her brow furrowed. 'You don't mind?'

'I'd rather you took a different view. We would find much pleasure together.' Pink bloomed in her cheeks, darkened and spread, as he held her gaze.

Her blushes delighted him. The illusion that she was virtually untouched, untutored in the realms of sexual passion, held a strange appeal. He wondered if the blush extended down across her breasts to her peaked nipples.

'You asked what I wanted and I told you. But as you don't want an affair, let us concentrate on our lunch.'

'As simple as that?' Disbelief echoed in her tone.

'As simple as that.' It was a good thing she didn't know how badly he wanted her. How intense was his desire. How eagerly he anticipated her eventual capitulation.

'But surely…' Frowning, she shook her head again as if to clear it. 'It would be better if I left.'

'Not at all. I'm looking forward to your opinion on our local fare.' He turned to reach for a plate.

'Still, I should go.' She made to rise and Arik fought the impulse to snare her hand.

'And your painting? You wish to leave that too?'

That stopped her in mid-movement, her expression arrested. But only for a moment. 'That's all right. I wasn't sure it would turn out well anyway.'

'You're a very bad liar, Rosalie. Has no one told you that before? Of course it's good. It's more than good.' He knew enough to understand Rosalie Winters had real talent.

'Nevertheless—' the jut of her chin sharpened '—it's only a painting. It's not worth…'

'You think I ask you to prostitute yourself for the sake of a painting?' Okay, so he'd used her art to get close to her. But pride rebelled at her idea that he'd blackmail her into bed. The doubt in her eyes fuelled his anger, tightened the muscles across his neck and shoulders.

'I am not quite as needy as *that*, Rosalie.'

'I didn't mean to insult you.' Her voice was a muffled whisper, yet she met his eyes. 'But I don't know you.'

Curtly he nodded. Women needed to protect themselves.

'Let me assure you, on my word as sheikh of my people, I would never force you into intimacy. If my own scruples aren't enough, remember I'm a public figure. Any wrongdoing on my part would swiftly become widely known.'

He watched her troubled face and, for a moment, wished he hadn't told her what was on his mind. It was too soon.

'I have never taken what was not freely offered.' He paused, letting her weigh his words.

Her eyes, shadowed and doubting, held his. He was losing her. The sudden appalling notion crowded his brain and he felt as if someone had punched him hard in the gut.

The intensity of his reaction didn't make sense. For all her intoxicating allure she was just a woman. There would be plenty of those when he returned to his normal life. Women eager and impatient for his attention.

Why did his heart thud harder as he waited for her to say goodbye?

'I *would* rather finish.' Her gaze slid from his as she half turned to watch the waves shushing in on the beach. 'But it wouldn't feel right, knowing you want more.'

He shrugged as relief hummed through him. 'Men often look and want. But we don't always get what we desire.'

His experience was different; he made it his business always to get what he wanted. No need to tell her that.

Her head swung round and their eyes met. He felt the impact in his tightening lungs. He wanted to thread a hand through the shimmering silk of her hair and pull her close. He wanted to taste her, not her hand this time, but her lips: lush, ripe, inviting. He wanted to explore her body, discover the places that triggered delight and ecstasy.

Slowly he exhaled. Patience. It would take time to breach the barrier of her distrust. She was as flighty as a newborn colt. Easily scared.

He summoned a smile and held out a plate. 'Let's enjoy lunch before it spoils. I will bring my horse to the beach each morning while you paint. In the afternoons we will view the local sights. Simple. No strings attached.'

*Simple*, he'd said.

Rosalie stared out the window of the four-wheel drive and knew this was anything but simple. All afternoon as they'd toured the old town, she'd struggled against the force of his personality, his magnetic attractiveness. Against desire and a burgeoning curiosity that undermined her determination to keep her distance.

She was losing the fight.

She should have left him at the beach. No matter that she *wanted* to feel it again, that rush of excitement when he looked at her with such searing intensity.

Perversely, it was his anger that had made her stay. The fury in his jet-dark eyes. Arik Ben Hassan had been genuinely outraged at the suggestion he might force his attentions. Pride had made his head jerk up, his eyes narrow in flashing denial and his hands curl into fists.

Rosalie wondered if the idea was outside his code of ethics. Or was it the hint that he might need to coerce any female to succumb to him? No doubt he cut a swathe through women with his looks and air of lazy sensuality.

Either way, she'd known with absolute certainty that he wouldn't use force. He might tempt and persuade, but he'd respect her wishes. She was safe: while she wanted to be.

The thought sent a skitter of feral excitement down her spine. Did he guess how she felt?

'I like the way the new buildings in the city blend in with the old,' she said abruptly, conscious that the silence had lengthened between them as he drove.

'I'm glad you approve. Planning sympathetic redevelopment has been a major issue for us.' His smooth voice drew her skin tight and tingling.

'You're involved in the planning?' She cut him a curious sideways glance.

He shrugged broad shoulders as he manoeuvred round a tight curve. 'I am the Sheikh. It is expected.'

She'd seen that amazing house, the obvious wealth he commanded, but hadn't considered the responsibilities of his position. Silly, considering what she knew of her brother-in-law's punishing workload.

'I suppose your official duties keep you busy.'

'Busy enough. But my work often takes me away.'

He had a *job* too? She'd imagined him living the good life, flitting from city to city, and woman to woman.

His dark eyes danced as he turned to her. His lips curled up in a smile that made her insides liquefy. How did he do that with just one slow, sexy grin?

'You're surprised I work?' He turned back to the road.

'I...suppose I assumed that you didn't need to.'

He nodded. 'But inactivity does not suit me. I couldn't loll about growing fat and idle.'

He'd never be fat. He had too much vigour. Even in repose his lean body was a study in power and leashed energy. She blinked and watched the road rather than let her gaze drift appreciatively over him.

'What sort of work do you do?'

'I manage a resources enterprise.' His deep voice sent a trickle of warmth down her spine.

'An oil company, you mean?'

'Oil and other things. We invest in renewable energy too. We're even experimenting in generating electricity from the sea.'

'You're not content to make your money from oil?' She'd heard Q'aroum had enough reserves to maintain it as one of the world's wealthiest states for generations.

'We're an island nation, Rosalie. We have a vested interest in combating climate change and rising sea levels. Besides, a man needs a challenge.'

His tone hinted that he wasn't just talking about power generation. Or maybe it was the sudden wide white grin that slashed across his face as he shot her a look.

She felt the whole impact of his personality focused on *her*. It was a tangible thing, a potent force. There was a rushing in her ears, like water flooding past, blocking the sound of nearby traffic. The late afternoon sun seemed to dim as she stared back at him, aware of her skin prickling on her neck and her lungs squeezing tight.

She had to be careful with this man. The feelings he evoked were too much. Too potent. Too new. Too tempting.

'I'll have you back to your hotel soon.'

She opened her mouth to explain that she wasn't staying at a hotel and then snapped it shut. Better if he didn't know she was staying alone in the house Rafiq had organised.

Arik had been a perfect gentleman all afternoon. Yet there was a restlessness about him, an edginess that warned her he wasn't as easygoing as he seemed. Something simmered behind that relaxed expression. Self-preservation cautioned her against revealing where she was staying.

'Thanks,' she said as they approached one of the two hotels on this coastal road. 'You can drop me here.'

'I'll see you to your door.'

Rosalie sucked in a deep breath. 'I'd rather you didn't.' He stopped the car and regarded her through narrowing eyes, his brows rising.

'You're not exactly incognito.' She remembered the excited pleasure with which he'd been greeted wherever they went. 'So I'd rather go in alone.' She wondered if he saw through her subterfuge. It was true as far as it went. She *didn't* want to draw attention to herself.

'Very well.' He inclined his head. 'We will not court gossip.' Then he got out and fetched her canvas bag from the back while she fumbled with her seatbelt.

His hand was warm and hard as he helped her out. A tremor shot up her arm at his touch, ripping right through any illusion that she was impervious to him.

'Thank you for the pleasure of your company, Rosalie.'

He lifted her hand to his lips. Her eyelids flickered as he pressed a kiss there. A jolt of something very like lightning speared through her. The swirl of reaction in her abdomen grew to a spiralling twist of aching emptiness.

It lasted an instant, only that. But it was enough to jolt Rosalie back to her senses.

She tugged back her hand as if stung. That empty yearning feeling was too real, too powerful to be safe.

'Until tomorrow, then.' His eyes were fathomless, deep as the night and just as impenetrable.

Rosalie turned away. Tomorrow, if she had any sense, she'd take the first flight out from here.

She was late. Arik narrowed his eyes against the slanting rays of dawn light and stared down the beach.

Had he erred yesterday? Should he have pressed his advantage when he'd read the need so clear in her eyes?

No. He'd given his word he'd respect her wishes. She was nervous, fighting to resist what was between them. As if she could push back the inevitable flood-tide of desire.

He wondered at her naïvety. Their attraction had been instantaneous, so urgent and all-consuming that even he, with his experience, couldn't ignore it. It was a constant fire in the blood, a gnawing hunger in the pit of his belly. He felt wired, restive and alert. Sleep was elusive, replaced by hours imagining her in his bed. Or naked, almost anywhere: in the window seat of his room, on a silk-covered divan or down here on the fine-grained sand.

The only way out was to assuage this need for mutual satisfaction. His lips curved in a taut smile. *Prolonged* mutual satisfaction.

Rosalie had much to learn and he would enjoy contributing to her education. Anticipation hummed through him, tightening his groin, his thighs, his hands on the reins. He nudged Layla till she gathered herself into a thudding gallop. The thunder of her hooves teamed with the beat of blood in his ears: heavy, urgent, racing.

They reached the point and there was Rosalie, walking from the next beach. Arik reined in, watching her falter to a stop. Her stance was wary, as if she were in two minds whether to scurry back to the safety of her hotel.

Eventually, as he'd known she would, she resumed her stride towards him. He should be pleased. Triumphant even.

He had her now, he knew. Or close enough that, with a little effort, he could have what he wanted from her.

Yet the emotion filling him wasn't triumph. It was fury. At the unprecedented level of his earlier disappointment. At the unadulterated relief that swept him now, making him for a few moments light-headed.

Since when had he been dependent on any woman? Pleasure, companionship, mutual enjoyment—that was what he sought from the women in his life. But this raw, visceral need that threatened all sense of proportion? That *drove* him with the force of pure compulsion? This wasn't right.

He watched her approach, her head up to meet his gaze, a gesture at odds with the defensive way she clutched that bag to her. Arik felt a surge of unexpected protectiveness.

But it was overborne by anger that she should unsettle him so. He was aroused to the edge of pain just watching her. And his indecisiveness as he'd debated ringing her hotel had been uncharacteristic. He was *too* needy.

Lust had never been like this. It *shouldn't* be like this. It had always been a pleasure to be savoured. Now for the first time, desire was a blood-deep craving. As if more was at stake than the pleasure of a woman's body. As if he felt far more than physical need.

Arik clenched his jaw at the absurd notion, angrier still at that flight of fancy. He urged his mount forward.

Rosalie wished she'd stayed away. What did it matter if her painting remained unfinished? Or if she never saw him again? She knew now that with effort she would paint. And as for her reaction to *him*…better to ignore that.

Yet like a moth to a candle she was drawn against her will along the beach. With every step she'd known this was dangerous, the sort of impetuous act she'd always avoided.

*But then*, a demon inner voice taunted, *where did playing safe get you*? She'd been perennially sensible, so cautious with men, and look where that had landed her!

She clasped her bag closer, wondering yet again how big a mistake she was making.

Then she saw him, a study in masculine grace and arrogance as he sat his magnificent Arab mount. Instantly she had her answer. Error or not, she couldn't have stayed away. The rapid-fire tumult of her pulse, the constriction of her lungs, the swirling heat all told the same story. She *had* to be here. Owed it to herself to discover what it was about this man that spoke to her innermost being, to the self she'd kept hidden for years now. The self that, at nineteen-and-a-half, had been brutally silenced, locked away by the force of grief and hate and despair.

More than three years had passed and suddenly that other Rosalie Winters, the one who'd secretly yearned for fantasy and adventure, was back, slipping under her guard.

She gritted her teeth and resumed walking. Foolish she might be, but she'd never again be the unthinking innocent she'd been at nineteen. She'd learned her lesson well. If she took any chances they'd be on her terms.

Nevertheless, as Arik's horse plunged close, its hooves lifting high to a resounding rhythm, she couldn't repress a thrill of mixed trepidation and excitement.

'I thought you weren't coming.' His deep voice held a note of accusation as it rumbled in her ear.

'I almost didn't,' she replied, annoyed as he circled. Man and beast together were awesomely beautiful—as he knew. He probably stayed up there so she could admire him.

That was the sort of man he was, she reminded herself, ignoring yesterday's revelations. She squashed the fact that he worked hard despite his wealth. Easier to deal with Arik Ben Hassan if she could peg him as a rich playboy.

Yet she followed his every move with hungry attention. He

was so vibrantly male, so attractive. Her imagination hadn't embroidered a single detail. He was devastating.

'You would have reneged on our bargain?' His expression was severe, as if no one ever had the temerity to inconvenience him.

Rosalie stepped away, preferring not to dwell on the fact that he could read her so easily. 'It's only a temporary arrangement. I wouldn't have thought you'd mind.'

He swung the mare round to walk beside her. 'I'd have minded very much,' he murmured and, despite her best intentions, Rosalie found herself looking up into midnight-dark eyes. Tension pulsed between them, the sizzle of unspoken connection that had no parallel in her experience.

'Then you should be pleased that I'm here after all.'

For two heartbeats he held her gaze, then the shadows fled. He smiled and something tumbled over in her chest at the zap of magnetism between them.

'And so I am, Rosalie. Very pleased.' His voice dropped to a deep sultry murmur that reverberated in her bloodstream, tingled through her body and awakened every nerve-ending.

Why, oh why, hadn't she stayed away?

*Because you've never felt so incredibly alive as you do here, with him.*

'You're not having second thoughts, are you?' He dismounted to stand beside her on the sand. With only a metre between them the space seemed too intimate.

'Perhaps. Should I?'

He shook his head and reached out, his fingers closing around hers, hard, warm and strong. It felt so right.

'No.' He tugged gently, bringing her closer. She saw herself reflected in his eyes. 'I will never hurt you. You have my word of honour.' Her thudding heartbeat echoed the pulse throbbing at the base of his neck. 'Trust me?'

She hesitated. She had nothing but his words and her instincts to guide her. Yet there was no doubt in her mind.

'Yes. I trust you, Arik.'

'Good.' A spark of emotion flared in his eyes, his hand tightened around hers and a wave of excitement washed over her. His gaze snared hers and her breath crammed in her throat at the intensity of his expression. 'You know what I want, Rosalie, but that must be your decision.'

She shook her head. 'But I've told you that I won't—' Her words ended on a hiss of indrawn breath as he lifted her hand to his mouth and pressed a kiss to the back of it.

'Perhaps you may change your mind.' His mouth moving against her skin was subtly erotic. She stiffened her spine against the need to slump in a wanting heap at his feet.

Now was the time to turn away and make her excuses. She wasn't sophisticated enough to play these provocative games of seduction. 'I'm not sure…'

Her words petered out into a sigh as he turned her hand and planted a tender kiss on the centre of her palm. A kiss that sent shockwaves of heat spearing through her. Her knees trembled at the force of them.

'Nothing is sure,' Arik murmured, caressing her with his lips as he spoke. 'Can we not simply enjoy each other's company for a few days and see where it leads us?'

*To perdition, probably.* Rosalie sucked a huge breath into her starved lungs, but it wasn't enough to restore her equilibrium. Not when his hot breath hazed her skin and his lips hovered a bare centimetre from her throbbing pulse.

She tugged her hand free and whipped it behind her back, terrified she might beg him to kiss her there again.

'You'll be disappointed.' She might be desperate for his caresses, but she wasn't completely foolhardy.

'Then so be it.' His smile gave nothing away.

The morning disappeared rapidly once Rosalie focused on her work and not the insidious twist of excitement low in her belly, testament to Arik's lethal attraction. But now and then, as she looked across the beach, his head would lift, his eyes meet hers and she'd feel the heavy throb of awareness in the crisp morning air.

Too soon the morning was over. Her canvas was taken to Arik's home. They'd eaten lunch and now they were alone in the opulent marquee that passed for a beach shelter. For all their small talk about art and local sights, Rosalie was acutely conscious of their isolation. The undercurrents eddying in the lengthening silence unnerved her.

She shot him a look, relieved to find that for once his attention was elsewhere. He seemed absorbed in the view of sea and sand, the distant blue shadow of an island.

His profile was arresting, etched with stark, sure lines comprising a whole that was more than handsome. There was intelligence in his high brow, or perhaps that was because she'd learned how perceptive he was. His eyes were piercing, unsettlingly so when they rested on her. His mouth—there was something innately sensual about the curve of his lips—the way it quirked readily into a smile that invited shared laughter. Or pleasure.

Her stomach dipped. He was a man who understood physical pleasure. It was obvious in the way he caressed her hand, the sensuous light in his eyes when he spoke of desire. His look held a promise of gratification. And, if she wanted, he could share that knowledge, that expertise with her. She had only to say the word and Arik would take her to places, to pleasure, so long denied her.

The knowledge was heady, tempting. Frightening.

How could she even consider his proposition?

*Because you're lonely. Because there's something missing in your life. Because there's something about this man that overrides a lifetime's caution and makes you long for the passion you've never had.*

She looked at him and she felt hot. Her skin prickled as if it no longer fitted. Her lungs couldn't process enough oxygen. There was a tingling, heavy sensation inside that kept her on edge, an aching sense of emptiness.

Suddenly his eyes were on her. Dark and gleaming with a heat that scorched her skin to a fiery blush. He knew what she felt, she realised in amazement.

*He understood.*

She read the reflection of her own burgeoning need in the haunted expression of his eyes. In the tic of a pulse at his jaw. Even the compressed line of his mouth mirrored the confused tension pulling her body taut.

His lips curved up in that sexy crooked smile but there was no humour in his gaze this time.

'You feel it too.' His voice was low and sure, sending a ripple of reaction through every nerve. 'You feel what's between us, don't you, Rosalie?'

She shook her head in denial. But she couldn't pull her gaze from his. It was as if some force trapped her.

'There's no need to lie,' he said and there was a glimmer of amusement in his look. 'You won't be singed by a bolt of lightning for admitting the truth. There's nothing shameful about desire between a man and a woman.'

Rosalie's breath caught high in her throat as his words echoed through her head. *Desire*.

He was right. That was exactly what she felt. Raw, unadulterated desire for the man before her. She shivered.

'But I'm not interested in becoming some playmate to keep a rich man from boredom.' It came out in a rush.

His stare hardened to a laser-bright glitter, keen and cutting. She'd gone too far. His face drew tight with repressed anger, accentuating his aristocratic bone structure. The pulse at his jaw raced to a frenetic beat.

She'd blurted out the first thing that came into her numbed

brain. But in this part of the world men called all the shots. Automatically she shrank back, expecting an explosion of outraged fury.

'You Australians believe in directness, don't you?' One dark brow winged up at an arrogant angle. Then he frowned, as if noticing her shuffled withdrawal.

Instantly his expression of stifled fury eased, replaced by a watching stillness.

'There's no need to be afraid to express your opinions.' His voice was calm but there was no mistaking its harsh rasping edge. As if he battled for self-control.

His eyes held hers and she knew he meant it. Relief relaxed her muscles. 'I'm sorry,' she said, wondering how he'd read her sudden fear. 'That was insulting.'

'You should not apologise.' His words cut across hers. 'You spoke the truth as you saw it.'

They stared at each other across the narrow space and once more Rosalie could have sworn he understood her confusion and fear. Understood far too much.

'I regret that you see my interest as cheapening.' He paused, as if the word left a sour taste. 'I have always regarded my love affairs as liaisons between equals.'

What could she say? Embarrassment flooded her but she could survive that. She'd survived much worse.

'Though I suppose,' he murmured, 'in this case it would be an unequal relationship.'

He was admitting it? Surely no man was that honest.

'After all, the power is squarely in your hands.'

'I beg your pardon?' Surely she was hearing things.

He shrugged those impressive shoulders. 'Don't be naïve, Rosalie. I want to become your lover.' His voice dropped so low that she felt it resonate deep inside, creating a hollow, wanting ache. 'I've said I won't do anything you don't want me to. I'd stop at a single word.'

His eyes were so bright now they seared her.

'So that means *you* have all the power in this relationship. You can ask for what you want. *Whatever* you want. And I'll give it to you.'

There was no mistaking the look on his face. Sex. That was what he was talking about.

'But,' he continued, 'you only have to say no and I'd be obliged to stop.'

Rosalie drew in a shaky breath, aware of moist heat blossoming across her skin. She bit her lip, striving for control against the illicit thrill coursing through her.

She shouldn't want him. She didn't need any man. Especially one as self satisfied and knowing as this one.

But that didn't prevent a surge of excitement. She could ask for whatever she wanted. As much or as little as she chose and he'd respect her wishes. She'd be safe.

'That wouldn't be right or fair.' Her voice was breathless, unsteady. 'It'd be better if I left.' But how would she find the strength to walk away and not look back?

'I never took you for a coward, Rosalie.' His deep voice fell like a stone in the silence between them.

She jerked her head around. 'Just because I don't want to play these games doesn't make me a coward.'

'Doesn't it?' Again one superior eyebrow lifted in query. 'Then what are you afraid of, if not yourself?'

Rosalie sucked in a breath. She wasn't afraid. She was cautious. He was far beyond her league.

Why then, did the idea of intimacy with him appeal so much? Why this excitement at the notion of exploring those sensations and cravings she'd so long repressed?

Her mother had hinted it was unhealthy for her to avoid personal contact with men as much as she had. What would her mum say about the unrelenting forces building within her right now? The temptation to say yes?

'I'm not afraid,' she lied.

'Good.' He leaned towards her till her whole world was encompassed by the brilliance of his dark eyes, the strength of his powerful shoulders blotting out the view and the warmth of his body reaching out to her.

'It's not fear I want from you, Rosalie.' His words were warm against her cheek. But he came no closer. An invisible barrier remained between them. The protection of his promise. Power rested solely in her hands.

Black, burning eyes met hers. The flare of his nostrils told her he registered it too—the faint musky aroma. The scent of arousal. From her skin? From his?

And yet he didn't move.

'Ahmed will bring the four-wheel drive soon,' he said.

Rosalie swallowed and swiped the tip of her tongue over her bottom lip. His gaze flickered and held.

'Is there anything you want before he arrives?' His words were barely audible over the thunder of her pulse.

'No. Nothing.' Yet her voice sounded like a sigh of wind, an echo of the soft waves on the beach.

'Are you sure?' he whispered.

She bit her lip to prevent herself from saying anything stupid. Arik was seduction on two legs and she had precious few defences against him. 'No,' she muttered again.

'No, you don't want anything? Or no, you're not sure?'

He was close enough for her to feel encompassed by the sheer strength of the man. His hands were planted on either side of her hips, his fingers splayed across the rich fabric of the carpet. His chest was like a wall, pressing her back, despite the fact that he didn't touch her. His gaze held hers, like a bird enmeshed in a net.

'I…' The words died in her throat as she realised what she wanted. What she *craved* from him.

'A kiss, perhaps? Just one to satisfy your curiosity?' His

mouth curled up in a smile that stopped her pulse for a beat. 'Surely you've wondered what it would be like, just a simple kiss between us?'

If only he'd looked smug she'd have been able to summon the will-power to push him away. But there was only the glow of invitation in his eyes. The temptation to pleasure in his curving lips.

'Yes,' she heard herself whisper on a sigh of surrender. 'I've wondered.'

'Good,' he murmured. 'In that we are equals.' His smile faded. 'Relax, Rosalie. You are safe with me.'

He leaned even closer, paused with his mouth an infinitesimal fraction away. He waited long enough for her to absorb the scent of his skin, adjust to the power and heat of his body almost touching hers, for her to taste his breath on her lips and to want more.

Then he slanted his mouth over hers and the world disappeared into a whirling blur as he took her mouth with his.

# CHAPTER FIVE

SHE kissed like a virgin.

Her lips were soft, pliant, clinging as he brushed his mouth against hers. Yet when he opened his mouth to slide his tongue along her lips she shivered, retreating a little.

So sweet. So enticing. He leaned closer, careful to keep his hands firmly on the floor. This time when he invited her to open for him, her lips moved against his, mimicking the gentle persuasion of his caress.

Instantly a surge of blood shot simultaneously to his head and his groin. A jolt of fire ignited in his belly, blasting his careful restraint to smithereens.

But somehow he managed to contain the compulsion to ravish her mouth, to pull her close to his needy body and plunder her depths.

He coaxed her mouth open, increasing the pressure slowly. Her breath was fresh and warm, her lips like satin, the scent of her skin heady and arousing. There was no artifice about her, not even so much as a manufactured scent. Yet her delicate kisses, her seemingly untutored response, had him clenching his fists against the impulse to throw caution and restraint to the winds and simply take what he wanted.

He'd never known such fierce need. He *had* to have her. Every atom of his being screamed for her. She was a temptress such as he'd never known before. A houri who seduced not with practised arts but with a tentative, natural eroticism that was unsurpassed in his experience.

What had he got himself into?

He pressed closer, his kiss more demanding. She melted against him, her sigh a muffled surrender in his mouth and instantly his blood thrummed an imperative to conquer. To take.

Yet he mustn't touch. Not this time. This time he had to go slowly, not scare her into headlong retreat. She was skittish enough as it was. If he touched her the way he wanted to, palmed her breasts, learnt the firm curves of her body, discovered her secret femininity and tasted her flesh with his tongue, he wouldn't be able to call a halt.

Instinctively he knew she needed time.

He wondered how long he could hold out before the visceral need that gnawed at his vitals overcame the last of his scruples.

He pressed closer still, the peaks of her breasts grazing his chest for an instant, sending a judder of erotic sensation straight to his groin. His erection was a heavy fretful ache that surged into full-blooded readiness. A groan of pain, of thwarted need, rose from his chest but he ignored it, fisting his hands tighter till the circulation ebbed and his fingers ached.

He'd started this and he owed it to Rosalie, as a man of honour, not to finish it here and now with a quick frantic coupling, no matter the cost to his fast-shredding self-control.

Arik was all she'd dreamed he'd be. And more. The dance of his tongue against hers, languorous and innately seductive, the taste of him on her lips, the scent of his warm skin so close— it was a heady combination that blasted any logic right out of her brain. The sheer bombardment of physical pleasure assailing her senses made her dizzy.

She wondered how it would feel if he wrapped his arms

around her and drew her close to the aggressive heat of his body. She longed to know. Could almost imagine the heavy weight of his strong torso against hers.

Rosalie shifted, edgy with an aching, empty sensation that would only be satisfied with more. More of Arik. More of the magic he created just with his lips and tongue against hers.

He pushed closer, still not close enough, and she almost sighed with relief as she felt the soft luxury of piled cushions behind her. He adjusted the angle of his mouth slightly, giving even better access to hers, and she knew with a faint last coherent thought that surrender wasn't so bad after all.

If only he'd touch her, lift his palm to her face and stroke her there, as she longed to be touched.

But, despite the intensity of their meshed mouths, of the spiralling desire between them, he took no further advantage. Only their mouths met and held, in a kiss that contained all the potent intoxication of pure need.

The pressure built inside her until she could ignore it no longer. She lifted her hands, tentatively skimmed them between his heaving solid chest and her over-sensitive breasts, up to his shoulders. Her hands lingered there indecisively till she heard a sound like a low growl in her ears, felt him shudder against her hands.

Without thought she responded to his primal maleness, the raw sound of his desire. She cupped the heated skin of his neck, revelling in the hint of racing pulse she discovered, the smooth, enticing sensation of his flesh against her hands.

She speared her fingers up through his hair. It was like rough silk to her touch. She cradled his skull as she drew him closer. But still it wasn't enough. It would never be enough.

The primitive rhythm pulsing in her blood, drumming in the dark, hidden core of her body urged her on. She needed more.

Then Arik moved.

Not in against her body as she craved. Instead he pulled

back, ending the kiss so suddenly that her eyes snapped open
and she lost the comforting sensual darkness.

What had happened?

Her lips were swollen, throbbing with the force of his
mouth against hers. Her breasts were full and heavy, her body
weighted with a languor she didn't recognise. She blinked,
trying to bring him into focus. Trying to engage her brain.

He breathed deeply, as if starved of oxygen, and she felt
his breath on her sensitised skin. Maybe that was why she felt
dizzy, she was panting as if she'd run a marathon.

Her hands still held him close. The sensation of hard bone
and flesh and soft hair beneath her hands was exquisite. She
saw her raised arms, her hands clutching him and realised,
muzzily, that she should let him go. But her brain couldn't
seem to conjure the appropriate command.

She stared up at him. His was the strong, burnished face
of seduction. The epitome of every secret, scandalous desire
she'd ever harboured. His lips were fuller than before, from
the taste of her. The knowledge sent a thrill of excitement
straight through her. His eyes gleamed brighter than ever
under those heavy hooded lids, as if he understood her
yearning. His high cut cheekbones and the strong lines of his
jaw, even the slashing angle of his nose, seemed more pronounced, as if the flesh had been pared back to reveal only
stark desire.

If sensual need had a face, it was here: bold and utterly
captivating.

Against him, against her own rising need, her defences
were crystalline: transparent, brittle and easily splintered. She
felt them crack and shatter under the heat of his flagrantly
wanting gaze. But it was the force of her own desire that
finally destroyed them. The knowledge that, however wrong,
however dangerous, *this* was what she wanted. *This man.*

The epiphany was instant and complete. For all her fear,

her caution, her longing for a safe secure life, she couldn't escape the truth.

She wanted Arik. In the most elemental way a woman could want a man.

She should have been embarrassed, swimming up out of her sensual haze to discover that she'd succumbed so completely to him. That, without lifting a finger, he'd enticed her back to lie before him in a pose of wanton invitation. With his mouth alone he'd coaxed her into a new reality, where all that mattered was the present, the all-consuming hunger for sensual pleasure.

Later, she knew, she'd wince at the image of her hands clutching him close, a symbol of her complete abandonment.

If he'd been less trustworthy, if he'd taken advantage as he so easily could have, she might not be lying here fully clothed. The thought created a twist of horror deep in her belly. She'd invited trouble when she'd lost control. But, amazingly, Arik had retained his. He hadn't faltered in his promise of a kiss only.

Her eyes widened as she stared into the impenetrable blackness of his gaze. He wanted her. He'd spelled it out more than once. Yet he'd taken no more than she'd agreed to. Despite the fact that he could have plundered her for so much more than a kiss. Despite the fact that she'd wanted him pressed against her, his hands on her body, his arms pulling her close.

Her brow furrowed as her foggy brain worked through the implications. Her hands grew lax and slid down his neck, past the iron-hard tendons and scorching heat of his shoulders. The heavy thud of his heart pounding against his chest reinforced the knowledge of his arousal and her hands dropped away.

Even in the sudden delirium of her new-found physical desire, she would have called a halt—eventually, but probably too late, if he'd decided she was willing.

She could barely believe she'd let herself go so far.

He could have pushed her even further into intimacy. Could have taken all that he wanted with very little persuasion.

Yet he hadn't.

She stared up at him, the throb of her racing pulse deafening in her ears.

He was a man of his word, she realised.

Against all the odds she'd found a man who could be trusted, even against his own urgent desires.

After the dark phantoms that crowded her past, that should be impossible. *A man she could trust.*

Rosalie's chest tightened suddenly as if constricted by metal bands. Her breath sawed in her lungs and a ball of burning emotion rose in her throat. She tried to swallow it down, combating the searing ache at the back of her eyes.

Stupid to be upset now, when everything was all right. She was safe, after all. Unharmed. Untouched, but for the heady caress of his mouth against hers.

Yet the sharp pain of unharnessed emotions accelerated rather than dwindled. She gulped down hard on the knot of sensation as she blinked against her blurring gaze.

'Rosalie?' His voice was rusty, harsh. 'What's wrong?'

She shook her head. She couldn't speak. And no way could she explain the surge of emotions churning within her: the relief and incredulity, the self-disgust and remembered pain. There was more too, a tumble of pent-up feelings that had more to do with the past than with what had just happened. Somehow their kiss, the intimacy between them, had unleashed the demons she'd kept at bay for so long.

Rosalie bit her lip and turned away. She felt him move to give her more space. He probably thought she was off her rocker! To get teary over a kiss. A first class mind-blowing kiss, but still, as far as he knew, just a kiss.

She planted her hands against the richly patterned carpet of the floor and tried to concentrate only on what she saw. On the delicate whorls of colour in the stylised pattern of flowers and tendrils in the silk and wool. Flowing lines, clear ruby

tones with a fine tracery of azure and cream and indigo. Buds
and leaves and arabesques of gold.

'Rosalie.' His voice was lower this time, husky and deep.
She felt it roll across her shredded nerves, soft and powerful
as the surge of the tide.

Even his voice had the power to seduce!

'I'm sorry,' she murmured, finding her voice at last. 'I
just felt a little…faint,' she lied. How else could she explain
the unstoppable force of raw emotion that had hit her, just
when she was at her most vulnerable? She couldn't explain
it to him. She could barely understand it herself. She just
knew that she'd experienced something…wonderful. And
it wasn't just Arik's expertise at kissing or the taste of mutual enjoyment. It was the tentative rekindling of faith in
another.

It had been a long time coming. Until today she'd never
thought it would happen.

And it was overwhelming.

She lifted a hand and surreptitiously wiped away the tears
that had overflowed on to her cheeks. With her shoulders
hunched and her back to Arik, she hoped he wouldn't notice.
But she doubted he'd miss anything. His eyes were as keen
as an eagle's. Which meant she had to brazen it out.

'Here.' She looked down to see his squared hand hold out
a gilt-edged glass to her. 'Drink this.'

It was tropical fruit juice. Cold, sweetly tart and refresh-
ing. The everyday act of sipping and swallowing helped. So
did the immediate sugar boost. Slowly she drained it.

'Thanks.' She held the glass out, darting a glance at his set
face, and then away from his intense scrutiny.

'Are you ill?' Arik took the empty glass and placed it on the
table. 'Do you need a doctor?'

She shook her head and the wispy tendrils of bright hair

swirled round her face, framing features that were only gradually regaining some colour.

'No, I'm okay.' Her lips quirked up in a perfunctory smile that tugged at something in his chest. 'I just felt a little…'

'Faint,' he finished for her, angry at the frustration of knowing he wouldn't get the truth from her now. Worried for her. Whatever had happened, she wasn't going to trust him with it. But of one thing he was sure: Rosalie Winters hadn't been on the verge of a faint, however stunning their kiss. He'd still been reeling from the impact of her mouth opening like a flower beneath his, the sensation of her warm, seductive body relaxing into complete abandonment beneath him, when he'd seen the look on her face.

Tears, that was what he'd seen. Tears and a flash of something he couldn't pin down. Surprise? No, it had been stronger than that. Amazement? Horror?

Surely not. He could vouch for the fact that no woman he'd kissed had ever been horrified by him.

And that kiss had been completely mutual, after those first few moments when she'd hesitated. No way could she have faked that reaction. She'd been perfect. Responsive; almost innocently seductive and eager. So eager that he'd been tested to the limit, reining in his burgeoning lust. No woman had ever tasted that good or felt so inviting. And it hadn't been the piquancy of their almost-caress, of knowing he shouldn't, couldn't trust himself to hold her and stop at a single kiss.

No, there was something…different about kissing Rosalie Winters. Something that left him with a gnawing, unsatisfied hunger deep inside. Hunger for her body. But for more too— for her smiles and her confidence.

He stared at her averted profile, lost for an explanation as to why this woman affected him so. Yet this wasn't the time to fathom it out. There was something wrong. Badly wrong.

'Would you like me to take you back to your hotel?' He

hadn't known he was going to make the offer until the words spilled from his mouth. It wasn't what he wanted. What he wanted was a repeat of that kiss. And to explore a little further, to hold her in his arms and learn the secrets of her body. Taking her back would put an end to those plans. And yet it mattered more to him that she recover from whatever had upset her.

Just as long as it wasn't him. What would he do if he discovered it was *he* who'd made her cry?

'Thank you, but I'm all right. It was just a passing thing.' She flashed him a look from stormy grey-green eyes that cut right through him. He'd give so much to see the shadows fade from her face.

'I'd rather go sightseeing—' she paused and drew in a shuddering breath '—if the offer still stands?'

Arik knew a moment's uncharacteristic indecision. Instinct told him he should press for more information, uncover whatever it was she kept hidden, for he knew it was important. But selfishly he wanted to spend the afternoon with her. If he pushed for answers then she could take flight and leave.

'Of course the offer still stands. On one condition.'

Her widening eyes met his. He watched the tip of her tongue slip out and moisten her lips and wished he'd bargained for another kiss. The effect she had on his body was overpowering and immediate. Even now, worried about her, he was hard with lust.

'What's the condition?'

'That if you feel faint again I take you straight to a doctor.'

Her smile this time was genuine and its impact hit him hard in the solar plexus.

'Thanks, Arik, but I'm sure I'll be okay.'

Watching her lips shape his name had to be one of the most erotic things in the world. Especially now, when her mouth was swollen from kissing him. The taste of her was still in his mouth, an addictive flavour that heightened his appetite for her. He stared at her lips a moment longer, wishing the old custom of wearing a face veil still prevailed. It was too distracting watching her mouth, inviting and lush, and not being able to take it again.

'Come.' He rose to his feet and held out an imperious hand to her. 'I hear the four wheel drive. It's time we were on our way.'

For an instant she hesitated, her eyes on his outstretched arm, and then she reached out and let him fold his hand around hers. Good. The trust was there still. Arik ignored the rush of relief he felt as he tucked her hand into the crook of his arm and led her outside. She was where he wanted her and that was what counted.

Late sunlight slanted down into the broad courtyard and glinted off Rosalie's hair. As the afternoon had progressed and she'd become more engrossed by what she'd seen, she'd forgotten to push the strands back from her face or catch them up into her usual ponytail. Now her hair was a rose-gold halo, framing her delicate features. The perfect foil for her clear skin and lush pink mouth.

Arik leaned against a stone pillar, arms crossed as he watched her. It had taken a while but gradually the shadows had disappeared from her face. The tense grey glint of her eyes had faded, replaced by a deep jade-green as she'd forgotten whatever it was that had caused her so much pain.

He'd learnt that much about her, that her mood could be gauged by the shade of her eyes. Storm-grey for pain or anxiety. Green for pleasure.

Her eyes had glittered green as she'd stared up at him after their kiss. He could have drowned in those depths, had felt the rising tide of need tugging him closer so he could lose himself in her. It had only been the glint of sudden tears that had halted him.

There'd been pain there. And it bothered him that he didn't

know why. Could it have been their kiss? No. It had felt too right. Something from the past, then? He sensed that Rosalie Winters was a woman of secrets. And he knew an overwhelming urge to lay them all bare, uncover her mysteries and conquer her fears.

He'd been right to bring her here. She'd been at home almost from the moment of introductions. Obviously art had a language all of its own for most of the artists here had only rudimentary French or English and Rosalie's Arabic, though surprisingly well accented for a beginner, was basic. Yet she'd made herself understood. In fact he'd been superfluous after the first half hour. He'd retired instead to take tea with the director, to discuss the school's progress and its finances. Despite the funding arrangements that ensured the place ran smoothly, there were always more worthy initiatives for Arik's money to sponsor.

'It's getting late,' he murmured eventually, closing in behind Rosalie where she crouched beside a young mosaic maker. Her gaze was focused on the nimble play of the girl's fingers as she selected another tiny glass tile, fitting it delicately into the pattern.

At first Rosalie didn't hear. It was only when he let his hand settle on her shoulder that she looked up and brought him into focus.

'I'm sorry; have I taken too long?'

He shook his head. 'Not at all. It's a pleasure to see your enthusiasm. But the school will be closing soon and you'll want to phone your daughter.'

'It's *that* late?' She gave her watch a stunned glance. 'I hadn't realised.' Immediately she turned to the young woman beside her and, in a mixture of English and halting Arabic, expressed her thanks and good wishes. The girl smiled and told her how much she'd enjoyed sharing her work.

It took time to say their farewells but eventually they left, walking through the courtyard gates and out to the vehicle. Arik glanced at the lowering sun. Too late to suggest going elsewhere and he knew Rosalie would again reject an offer of an evening meal together. She was too wary about being alone with him. In fact, after her reaction to their kiss, he wondered if she'd find some excuse not to meet tomorrow.

'Arik?' Automatically he stopped at the sound of his name on her lips. Her voice was soft and tentative and a jolt of ice speared him at the thought that he'd been right. She was going to renege on their arrangement.

She stood beside him, her head just topping his chin, and he experienced a fierce urge to pull her close and not let her go, no matter what her objections.

'You didn't tell me that you funded the art school.'

He frowned, nonplussed at her words. Of all the things she might have said, that was the least expected. The frozen shard in his chest began to thaw as he relaxed.

'What makes you think I do?'

'One of the instructors mentioned it when he was showing me around.' She paused, staring up at him. 'You don't mind me knowing, do you? It's such a brilliant idea, fostering young talent and at the same time providing an education for kids whose families find it difficult to support them. I think it's great.'

He shrugged, repressing his annoyance that his role in the enterprise had been raised. It wasn't a secret; after all, he was involved in lots of schemes to support his people. 'I didn't bring you here to impress you with my work as a benefactor. I simply thought that, as an artist, you'd enjoy seeing the work of other talented artists.'

'And I *did*. It was wonderful. Especially the ceramic painters and the mosaic makers.' Her eyes shone with an enthusiasm that made her face glow. Her hand grasped his forearm, but he guessed she didn't notice.

He did. He felt the imprint of each finger through the cotton of his shirt, the warmth of her palm, and wanted more. The craving for her touch against his bare flesh was so strong he wanted to tear his shirt open and plant her palm against his chest. Right here, right now, in the lengthening shadows of the school grounds, he wanted her hands on him, stroking, clinging as he embraced her.

'I'd love to try mosaic work. But I don't know anyone with that sort of expertise at home to teach me.'

'You could learn here. Stay a little longer. There'd be no objection to your taking tuition here.'

Her head tilted back and her bright eyes met his. The force of their impact sent heat sparking through him.

'It's tempting but, no, I couldn't. I have responsibilities.'

Her daughter. Of course.

Suddenly the prospect of their short relationship ending, as it naturally would, loomed on the horizon, far too close. The thought unsettled him.

Could it be that he wanted more than a few days with Rosalie? More than the pleasure of her body for the time it took him to recuperate and resume his normal routine?

'Perhaps during another visit, later?'

She hesitated for a moment. Long enough for him to be appalled at how he hung on her answer. Did her presence mean that much to him?

'Maybe one day,' she said at last, slipping her hand away. 'In the meantime I need to work on my painting skills. I'm so rusty.'

'Then it's a good thing you have time in which to work on them.' He gestured for her to precede him towards the gate. 'We will meet at the same time tomorrow?'

'Yes, same time tomorrow.' Her voice was light and breathless, as if she were nervous. But that didn't bother him. She intended to meet him again, despite her…*faintness* earlier. His bloodstream fizzed in anticipation.

Whatever had happened to make her wary, Rosalie Winters kissed like a woman blind to everything but him. And he intended to capitalise on that enthusiasm. Very soon.

# CHAPTER SIX

ROSALIE looked around the huge room with its magnificent view over the sea and knew she'd stepped straight into a world of wealth that most people never experienced.

There was nothing gaudy or ostentatious here but Arik's home was imbued with the luxury only serious money could buy. Generation upon generation of riches and privilege. And hard fought battles, she realised, noting the pair of antique muskets mounted over an arched doorway. They were decorated with the finest silver embossing, making them fit weapons for a sheikh.

'It's breathtaking,' she said, turning slowly around. And it was. From the spectacular panorama along the coast to the superb silks of hand woven rugs and tapestries. From the fine-grained leather of low modern lounges to the high vaulted ceiling tiled in a mosaic the colour of lapis lazuli, complete with a sprinkling of golden stars.

'It pleases me that you approve of my home.' Arik was his usual urbane self as he watched her take in her surroundings. His eyes were unreadable, his tall body relaxed. Again she wished he wasn't quite such a perfect host. She longed for a glimmer of the passion she'd seen in him two days ago. That she'd felt in the erotic caress of his mouth against hers.

Heat burned across her cheeks at the memory and she swung round towards the wide terrace that hung out over the cliff.

The memory of Arik's kiss. She'd been unable to put it from her mind. Or forget her reaction to it.

She'd gone to the beach the following day, half nervous, half secretly thrilled at the thought of him kissing her again. This time he'd pull her close in his arms, let her feel his strong body against hers, alleviate her burgeoning curiosity to know his touch.

She'd gone expecting another lesson in seduction from this man who was obviously a master of the art. She hadn't even considered not going—and that was the most telling thing of all. Despite her past, despite the fact that she hadn't trusted a man in years, the need to see Arik again, to be with him, overrode all else.

Perhaps, as her mother promised, time *did* heal. Maybe she was ready to take a chance on life.

Rosalie stared through the plate glass doors to the terrace and, beyond that, the vivid aquamarine of the sea.

It had been a momentous thing for her, deciding she wanted what Arik offered: the chance to experience passion, to ease the unceasing hollow ache deep inside her that told her she wanted a man—wanted *him*. That had been a revelation of her own femininity. Proof that she really *had* moved on from her troubled past.

In the long ago days when she'd indulged in daydreams she'd pictured a future with a man by her side. Someone she could rely on, who'd love her always. But times had changed and she knew that what Arik offered was perfect for her now: a way to explore her feelings, assuage these new found sexual cravings in safety. For he would be tender. He could be trusted.

And he was experienced enough to teach her all she longed to know. She shivered and crossed her arms at the thought of what she wanted from Arik.

Too bad he'd obviously changed his mind.

She was ready for more. But now he behaved like a perfect distant gentleman. He avoided so much as touching her hand, had clearly pulled back from intimacy. Dully she'd wondered if she'd kissed so badly that he'd decided she was no longer worth the effort of seducing. It wouldn't surprise her.

But he was a man to whom a promise was important and it seemed he was determined to stick to their bargain. Lunch yesterday had been a short affair. Then in the afternoon he'd driven her round part of the coast road, pointing out towns, historic sites and scenic vistas that should have caught and held her imagination. But she'd been too deep in disappointment to care.

How did you tell a man you wanted him to make love to you? Was it really that simple? And what if, like Arik, he'd clearly decided he was no longer interested?

Last night in her lonely bed had been the worst. She'd been so edgy she hadn't slept. Even after a long phone chat with her mother and Belle. Even after a relaxing bath. All that had achieved was to remind her that her body was…aroused. Ready for Arik's touch.

Heat scalded through her. Even now, after a second morning of polite decorum from Arik while she'd painted, she couldn't banish her craving for him. It was shaming, this relentless need, the breath-stealing suspense as she watched his every move and hoped he'd reach out to touch her.

Sensual awareness had come late to her and she hadn't yet mastered the art of controlling it. Why else was she standing here, breathless with the forlorn hope that even now, after two days of scrupulous distance, Arik might continue where their kiss had left off?

Blindly she groped for the door handle, swung open the glass door and stepped out. She needed air. She needed sanctuary. She'd been an idiot to agree when Arik had suggested they lunch at his home today. What she really needed was to get away while she had some shred of self-respect left.

She leaned heavily on the stone balustrade, her fingers gripping tightly, her chest constricting as she fought for control.

Laughable, wasn't it? Finally to decide to take up Arik's seductive promise of a no-strings affair and then to discover the option was no longer on offer. She shook her head miserably. Just another of life's disappointments.

In the overall scheme of things, this surely didn't rate such profound regret.

'Rosalie?' He stopped just a pace behind her and saw the tension stiffen her spine when she realised he was so close. The sea breeze fanned her hair and he shoved his hands deep in his pockets rather than reach out and fondle the silken tresses.

'It's a magnificent view. You're so lucky to have this.' Her gesture encompassed not only the beach far below but the ancient fortress that was his home. Yet he was more interested in the high uneven tone of her voice and in her averted profile.

She was doing it again, shutting him out.

Damn it! After two days of superhuman restraint, he deserved more. He'd read the pain so clear in her expression after their kiss and he'd respected her need for space. It had almost killed him, reining in the drive to claim her. To bind her close in his arms and not let her escape till he found satisfaction. That kiss, a mere taste of her treasures, had only titillated.

He needed more. Far more.

What had begun as an idle amusement had become a raw compulsion. He'd recognised her wariness, her fear, and gone slow. But he'd seen the hot desire in her unconscious responses and now it was time to act.

'Yes, extremely lucky.' He took another step towards her, close enough to feel the heat she generated and hear the hasty breath she sucked in. 'My ancestors fought long and hard to win this territory and keep it safe for their people.'

'And now you enjoy the benefits.'

Still her head was averted. Was she afraid of what he might read in her face? The thought spurred him. He leaned forward and placed one hand on the balustrade beside hers. There was a neatness to it—her hand, small and delicate, yet, he knew, clever and capable, beside his own. She'd be like that all over: skin pale and soft, dainty and feminine. In his mind's eye he could picture his own darker, larger hand moving slowly across her bare flesh, sliding, caressing, discovering. He could almost hear her sighs as he located each sensitive spot on her body and claimed it for himself.

'I make it my policy always to enjoy the benefits on offer.'

Her head swung round then, her eyes wide and confused. Her lips parted and he wanted to duck his head and taste her. Instead he took a slow breath and reached for her hand. It slid into his unresistingly and he felt his mouth kick up in a tight smile of satisfaction.

'Come, Rosalie. Our lunch will be ready. You can admire the view later.'

She was silent as he led her into the house. Silent as he took her through room after room, giving her a potted history of the fortress-cum-palace that had been built by one of his ancestors hundreds of years ago. He had no idea if she took in his words; he barely registered them himself. He was more absorbed in the feel of her, hand in his, the proximity of her so close beside him as he took her deeper into the palace.

'Your home is huge,' she said at last as they approached the end of a long passageway.

He didn't tell her that they'd eschewed the public dining rooms, all three of them, in favour of a meal in his private suite. Even with his well-trained staff, he had no intention of being disturbed this afternoon.

His fingers tightened fractionally round hers, then released their grip as he gestured for her to enter his chambers.

'After you, Rosalie.'

For an instant her eyes lifted to his and he felt the now familiar jolt, like a bolt of electricity, sizzle through him.

Then she stepped over the threshold and into the suite. He fought to keep the anticipatory smile from his face.

Her exclamation of delight masked the soft click of the door closing behind them and he turned to see her standing in the deep semi-circular window embrasure that jutted out over the cliff-line. She reached out to brush her hand across the continuous round seat that lined it and then lift to the silk hangings, tied back to reveal the view.

His body thrummed an urgent message of need. He'd imagined her here so often, naked on that padded seat, or leaning back against the window frame, her bare arms out-stretched invitingly towards him. The images were almost his undoing. Tension knotted his muscles and he felt the strain of imposing control in every cell of his body.

Deliberately he turned away and walked further into the sitting room, towards the drinks tray positioned beside one of the sofas.

'Would you like a cool drink?' he murmured in a voice rough with repressed desire.

'Yes, please.'

He glanced over his shoulder and found she'd moved, by-passing the circular table laden with food, and was investigat-ing the large telescope positioned before the next window.

'You look at the stars?'

He shrugged, remembering the day—was it only a week ago?—when he'd first seen her through the telescopic lens. He'd known even then what he'd wanted from her.

'Or the ships at sea. There's a lot of activity in the shipping lane further off the coast.' He put ice in a couple of glasses, then filled them. 'I was in plaster with a broken leg and looking for any diversion. I'm not used to being cooped up.' He turned and offered her a glass.

'How did you do it? Break your leg, I mean.'

'An accident on an oil rig. It happens. But, fortunately, not often.' An explosion on a rig was disastrous. And this time it had nearly claimed the life of one of his men. If Arik hadn't realised in time and turned back to look for him as they'd been evacuating, they might have had a fatality on their hands instead of mere fractures.

'It sounds dangerous.' She looked up at him so seriously that he wanted to pull her close and reassure her. But he couldn't take her in his arms. Not yet.

'Most of the time it's no more dangerous than being on land. It was just a matter of bad timing.' He turned towards the table that almost filled the window embrasure. 'It looks like Ayisha has been busy.'

'Ayisha?'

'My cook. She seems to have decided we must be starving after our exertions on the beach.' From the corner of his eye he saw Rosalie start. He wondered if, like him, she'd been thinking of exertions other than riding and painting. The suspicion pleased him. 'I hope you're hungry.'

Personally he was ravenous. But not for food. At least the meal would force him to take his time and not ravish her immediately. 'Please, take a seat.'

He watched Rosalie settle on the wide padded seat beneath the windows and then pushed the round table in closer, within easy reach. He slid in beside her, close but not touching, and placed his untouched drink on the table.

The food was delicious. Subtly spiced, fragrant with herbs and unnamed spices, melting in the mouth at each bite. And yet Rosalie found it almost impossible to concentrate on the fare before her.

Instead it was the man at her side who took all her attention. Surreptitiously she watched his strong hands reach for dishes, lift covers, offer delicacies. A shiver slid across her skin as his fingers brushed hers. She loved his touch, had secretly dreamed of it all over her body. Now the sight of his hands mesmerised her into a haze of fascination and longing. She wanted to reach out and draw Arik's hand closer, close it over her breast so she could feel its strength against her softness.

Rosalie swallowed down hard on a morsel of grilled fish and tried to concentrate on the meal.

She listened to his stream of small talk that reinforced the leisurely tempo of the meal. But there was no way she could relax. As each moment passed the tension in her stomach notched harder, tighter.

Arik passed her some rice flavoured with apricots, raisins and almonds.

'This is one of Ayisha's specialities and I can recommend it. Would you like some?' The flash of his smile stole her breath and she found herself nodding, even though her throat had closed and she doubted she'd be able to swallow properly.

'Here,' he murmured, his voice dropping to a low, husky pitch that seemed to reverberate right through her, 'tell me what you think.'

He lifted a fork laden with fluffy rice and held it out. Eyes as dark as her own midnight longings looked back at her and she felt something loosen and give way, deep inside her. Restraint? Caution?…Fear?

Obediently she opened her mouth, catching the flicker of expression in his eyes, unable to place it. She was too wrapped up in the…intimacy of having this man feed her to even try.

Taste exploded in her mouth—sweet, nutty, a perfect blend of flavours. But it was his gaze that had her attention. It was a palpable force, warming her skin, holding her still, waiting for his next move.

Finally she swallowed. 'It's delicious.'

'Good.' His one-sided smile sent a surge of pure longing through her. 'Have some more.'

Again he held out the fork. Again he watched her open her

mouth and accept the food. And once again she saw a ripple of something in his expression. Something at odds with the easy, relaxed pose of his big body and the slow smile on his face.

Hurriedly she chewed and swallowed. 'Thank you. But no more.'

He raised one lazy dark eyebrow in enquiry. 'You've had enough?'

Silently she nodded.

'Ah, then we come to my favourite part of the meal.'

Something about the low burr of his voice, the infinitesimal strengthening of his accent, made gooseflesh rise on her skin. She shivered.

'Really?'

He inclined his head, still focused on her in a way that made her conscious of the heavy beat of her pulse, the miniscule distance separating them.

'Dessert,' he said. 'I've always had a weakness for sweet things.'

The words were innocuous. But not the way he said them. She *knew* he wasn't merely discussing food. His very look was an invitation: flagrant, tempting.

Now was the time to leave. To say she really needed to be going. That she'd changed her mind and wanted to go home. Or that she had a headache. Anything to get her out of here, where this man's ability to seduce with a look, a word, was the most potent force she'd ever known.

She could do it. She knew she could. If she wanted to.

'I...'

'Yes, Rosalie?' He leaned a fraction closer—close enough for her to inhale the scent of his skin: hot, male, musky.

She licked her lips. This was her chance to escape back to safety. Arik wouldn't stop her; she knew that with absolute certainty. She could scurry away to her private refuge from the world, turn her back on temptation and rely on the lessons of fear and caution she'd learned in the past three years. They would protect her from hurt.

'I like dessert,' she whispered after a long pause.

Immediately she was rewarded with the bright blaze of his smile, radiant with approval.

'And you shall have it, Rosalie.' His voice was lower, throatier than before, and she started when he reached for her hand, raised it to his mouth and placed a single kiss to the back of it. His thumb stroked her sensitive skin and she shuddered as awareness prickled through her, from the sensitive tips of her breasts to her neck, her thighs and deep in her womb.

He turned her hand and pressed a kiss to her palm, let his tongue lave its centre, and a jolt of something white-hot and stunning burst through her. She felt a clenching deep inside as every nerve reacted. Automatically she tugged her hand, trying to break his grip, but he simply smiled and held both her hands in his.

'There is no need for haste. We have all afternoon.'

Then he released her hand and reached out to a platter at the centre of the table.

'Would you like some fruit?'

She stared at the plate, her mind slow, still catching up after the effect of Arik's smile on her nervous system.

'I…yes. Thank you.' Her throat was dry, her voice cracked. She took refuge in a gulp of her iced juice as she frantically tried to get a grip on her churning emotions.

Had she done the right thing? Was she regretting the impulse to stay?

She waited for the icy finger of fear to trail down her spine, for the churning regret to unsettle her stomach.

But all she felt was a hot eagerness. An avid expectation that soon, very soon, she'd be in Arik's arms. She bit down on the small secret smile that curved her lips at the thought.

No, she had no regrets.

'Peach?' he offered and she turned her head. He held up a neat sliver of fresh fruit to her. It smelled like summer and it tasted like sunshine as she let him slip it between her lips. There was the faintest brush of his fingers against her mouth and then his hand was gone.

Her lips tingled from that fleeting touch.

'Aren't you having any?' she said as he held out another piece to her. This time his touch lingered against her mouth a second longer. Time enough for her to take in the slight salt tang of his skin and feel the passing caress of his thumb against her bottom lip.

Heat bloomed deep inside. Darts of sensation shot through her, pulling her straighter in her seat, eager for his next offering.

'That depends,' he said, letting his gaze slide from her face to her hand, grasping the edge of the table in a white-knuckled grip.

Depends? Rosalie looked from her hand to Arik and then to the neatly sliced peach on the plate before her.

*It depends on me* she realised with a thrill of daring. Tentatively she reached out and picked up a wedge of fruit. It was ripe, slippery with juice, and her fingers trembled.

Did she really mean to be so…provocative as to feed him?

She took a slow breath, trying to regulate the rhythm of her racing heart. But when she looked up into his fathomless eyes, her pulse pounded harder than ever. His gaze was so intense that she felt it graze her features, brush over her throat and linger on her lips.

Rosalie offered him the fruit, the tremor in her hand so pronounced that she was barely surprised when he closed his fingers around hers while he slid the peach into his mouth. He chewed, swallowed, smiled, and then licked the juice from her fingers.

A shudder of pure longing swept through her. Her nipples peaked, pebble-hard against her bra as she watched him suck the sticky sweetness from her thumb, her forefinger. Incendiary heat shot straight to the pit of her belly and to the moistening core of her desire.

*Oh, my.*

'Delicious,' he whispered in a throaty voice so deep it resonated within her.

Still holding her hand, Arik selected another segment of peach and held it to her lips. This time he didn't draw his hand away and she had to slip it from between his fingers. Heaven! It tasted of him. Or did he taste of the fruit? His thumb pressed against her bottom lip and she slid her tongue along it, watching the glimmer of anticipation in his eyes. Cautiously she parted her lips a little wider and took his thumb into her mouth, sucking the sweetness from it.

The searing pleasure in his expression reflected her own excitement, told her this was a mutual delight.

That was a heady realisation. For the first time she felt a thrill of power, knowing she could affect him so.

He might be the master at this, but even the novice had something to offer.

She reached for another piece of fruit and felt an unravelling, unsettling sensation as she watched him eat from her hand, then use his tongue to swipe up the juice on each of her fingers.

Her eyelids drifted down on a wordless sigh. She felt…everything. Her skin had grown so sensitised that even the lap of his tongue over a fingertip, the caress of his lips on her palm, was enough to seduce her into ecstasy.

'Rosalie.' At the sound of his voice she opened her eyes and found him leaning closer, offering her another piece. Obediently she took the segment but she was clumsy and juice dribbled from her lips.

He still held her hand in his so she lifted her other one to wipe away the moisture. But she was too late. Already he'd moved, tilting his head to catch the droplet of juice with his tongue.

She shuddered at the sensual impact of his mouth on her

flesh, smoothing along her chin. She felt his breath on her, scented him in her short, urgent gasps and shut her eyes against the dizzying onslaught of awareness. He kissed her jaw line, the corner of her mouth, across the sensitive spot beneath her ear that sent arrows of heat to every nerve in her body.

Her head lolled back as he pressed his lips to her throat, evoking the most exquisite sense of abandonment. If he put his hands on her now she'd welcome his touch. Revel in it.

And then, suddenly, he was gone. Rosalie opened her eyes to find him watching her, so close that she had only to lean forward a little to bring her lips to his.

For a heartbeat she stalled in thought, wondering, wishing. And in that instant Arik moved, shifting back in his seat and half turning away.

Panic shot through her. Had he changed his mind? He must *know* she wanted him. She sat up straighter just as he turned and held out a small damp cloth.

His expression was tight, almost hard, as he wiped the cloth across her chin and then her hands, removing the last sticky traces of peach. Then he flung the linen on to the table and fixed his eyes on hers.

What she saw there stole her voice. Gone was the laid-back insouciance she'd come to expect from Arik. The teasing half smile. Even the enigmatic stare.

Now his face seemed cast in hard bronze, drawn tight with the force of a compulsion he couldn't hide. On any other man that look would have frightened her.

On Arik it excited her.

'It's time,' he said, reaching out and enfolding both her hands in his. 'You've decided, haven't you, Rosalie?'

He paused, awaiting her response. Words were beyond her, so she nodded.

'Good.' Already he was drawing her to her feet. 'At last we will be lovers.'

# CHAPTER SEVEN

THE light sea breeze from the open windows cooled Rosalie's flushed cheeks as he drew her through the arched doorway into his private domain. His bedroom was large, light and airy. At the centre of the back wall was a low bed, wide and sumptuous with its richly patterned coverlet. That was where Arik led her, slowly, inexorably, till it lay before them, a blatant invitation to pleasure.

She swallowed hard, faced with the reality of her desire. Did she have the nerve to go through with this?

But then Arik's hands were on her, gently compelling, drawing her down to the bed, and there was the promise of heaven in his touch. The lure of long-denied fulfilment. Of joy. Rosalie sank down beside him, leaning in against him without a second thought. For now it was her body responding, not her mind. She acted on instinct alone.

Their kiss was perfect. Growing passion tempered by a fierce restraint she sensed in him. And this time it wasn't just a meeting of lips and tongues. As he slanted his head to gain better access to her mouth, she felt his hands skim over her. Even through her clothes his touch ignited a desire that sparked and seared. Over the bare skin of her face and neck, across her shoulders, her back, her arms, down her sides and back up to her face. Wherever he caressed her he left a trail

of sizzling excitement. It burned across her skin, coiled hard
and tight inside her, till she was on fire, desperate for something to assuage the raging need.

Then the welcoming heat of his big body encompassed her,
the hard strength of bone and taut muscle.

Automatically she clung to him, revelling in the sensation
of his torso pushing her down into the soft mattress.
Breathlessly she registered the way his broad chest flattened
her breasts, but there was no pain, only a growing edginess,
a delicious awareness tingling through every centimetre of
her. She wanted to rub herself against him, explore his hard
muscled form with her hands, her lips, her body.

She wanted to imprint herself on him and to feel his flesh
against hers. She wanted...

'Rosalie.' His deep throaty murmur against the corner of
her mouth was enticing, seductive. Did she hear it or feel it?
His lips brushed her own, caressed the sensitive corner of her
mouth, dipped down to the pulse point low on her neck, and
she arched up involuntarily, gasping with delight.

The impact of that kiss reverberated to every pleasure point
in her body. There was effervescence in her blood, a surge of
energy so strong she felt almost faint with it.

'I've waited so long for you,' he whispered and now she
felt his hands move, deftly unbuttoning her shirt.

She opened eyes she hadn't realised she'd closed and stared
up at Arik. He was breathtaking, each severe line of his face,
each angle and plane contributing to a whole that was compelling. He was handsome, beautiful even, in a hard, ultra-
masculine way. But it was the inner fire, the spark of his
personality, and of his desire, that overwhelmed Rosalie.
There was a single-minded intensity about him that would
have scared her a week ago.

Now she revelled in it.

She wanted Arik so much. *Needed* him. His expression:

eyelids hooded, nostrils flared, mouth a taut line, made something leap inside her.

Then she registered the caress of cool air as he spread wide the sides of her shirt, baring her from the waist up to his gaze.

His eyes lingered on her bra, tracing its curve over her breasts. His gaze was smoky with desire.

'You are beautiful, Rosalie.' He lifted a hand and feathered his fingers along the upper edge of her bra.

She jolted at the unexpected intensity of that light touch. Her breath was a gasp of pure pleasure. Without thought she arched her back, silently begging him to repeat the gesture.

'And so exquisitely responsive,' he murmured as he again stroked the upper curve of her breasts and her eyes fluttered shut.

His tone was appreciative, knowing. It reminded her for an instant of the gulf of experience between them.

'I'm not protected,' she blurted out, then bit her lip as a fiery blush rose in her cheeks.

'Of course it will be my responsibility to protect you, little one.'

His gentle tone persuaded her to open her eyes. His gaze met hers and suddenly the embarrassment she'd felt a moment before was gone. She took a slow breath, saw the way his expression flickered at the deep rise of her breasts, but forced herself to go on.

'I don't have much…' *Experience*, she'd been about to say. But then she'd been pregnant, had given birth. He wouldn't understand. And she didn't want to enter into long explanations, not now. 'It's…'

'Been a while?' he finished for her, his gaze piercing. 'Don't worry, Rosalie. Once learned, the lessons of love aren't forgotten.'

That was what she was afraid of. Maybe she'd better tell him. She opened her mouth reluctantly but he forestalled her.

'Between us, little one, it will be easy.' His deep voice was reassuring and his slow smile reminded her that she could trust him. His eyes glowed with an excitement that matched her own. Could she ask for more?

Again his hand traced the outline of her bra, then dipped lower to find and tease her nipple through the cotton fabric.

She sucked in her breath in a hiss of surprised delight. Who'd have guessed such a touch would make her feel…?

'Perfect,' he murmured as he lowered his mouth to hers. 'It will be perfect with us.'

Then there was no more thinking. No more worries. No embarrassment. There was only the hot dark velvet of his kiss, the rising excitement as his hand grew heavier, more demanding at first one breast and then another.

She could grow addicted to Arik's touch. So sure, so sensitive. Her body clamoured for more, pushing up against his hand, his body, relieved and yet unsettled at the weight of him over her. It was what she wanted, but it wasn't enough.

When he drew back a fraction, her hands clung to his shoulders, her mouth throbbed from the passion that had soared between them. A passion reflected in the blaze of his eyes and the heave of his chest with every breath he took.

The last lingering shadow of doubt fled. She knew this was right.


'I want to touch you, Rosalie.' Arik was surprised at how steady his voice sounded. He teetered at the edge of his control, fiercely resisting the relentless urge to rip her clothes away and bury himself quick and deep in her soft waiting warmth.

He'd known urgent desire before, had more than enough experience to be able to temper his urges to ensure his partner was satisfied. Until now. The intensity of each sensation, the effect of watching Rosalie come alive at his touch, breathless and eager and somehow vulnerable, was something completely new to him.

His body felt as if it were on a rack, stretched almost to breaking-point by the weight of restraint placed upon it. Each muscle and sinew was stretched to the limit. But there was no alternative. He remembered the instant of doubt he'd seen in Rosalie's face and knew he had no choice but to love her slowly. Even it if killed him.

Gently he pushed her shirt from her shoulders. She shrugged out of it and he tossed it away.

'Touch me,' he ordered, hungry for the feel of her against his bare skin. For a moment she didn't move and then, slowly, so slowly he wanted to reach out and yank her hands against his chest, she reached up to him. Her fingers fumbled with a button. And then another. And then her hand slipped into his shirt, right over the spot where his heart pounded its message of hunger and painful control.

His eyes closed as he absorbed the sensation of her hand across his chest.

'More,' he demanded. The gentle exploration faltered and then, a moment later, her fingers worked his shirt buttons again. This time quickly, nimbly, and he sucked in a breath of relief. Another hurdle passed.

He waited till his shirt hung open, then shrugged his shoulders and shook it away. Opening his eyes, he found her staring, absorbed, as if committing to memory the sight of his bare torso. The look in her eyes did dangerous things to his ego. He felt like a hero, a god, not an ordinary man, when she looked at him like that.

She moved her hands over his chest, up and across, then circled down over muscles that spasmed at her touch. His arms trembled at the effort of remaining still under her caress.

'You're beautiful,' she breathed.

'No, Rosalie. But you are.' He couldn't resist the lure of

such temptation any longer. He reached out and slid his hand behind her, making short work of her bra clasp, drawing her plain white, ridiculously seductive bra away in his hand.

There was a hiss of frantic breath. A moment of stunned appreciation, and then he was touching her, stroking his index finger under the curve of her full, luscious breasts, up between them, then down and across the rose-pink nipples that tightened into buds at his touch.

She was exquisite. Perfect. And the little tremors vibrating through her at his caress were delicious proof of her incredible sensuality.

He palmed one breast, felt its weight in his hand, smiling at the exact fit. Hadn't he known she'd be just right? His fingers tightened on that sensitive bud, twisted just a fraction, and her whole body jolted.

It was as if she'd been waiting just for him. The thought was ridiculous, but an inviting fantasy, one he couldn't quite shake.

Her breath came in shallow pants, the sound of it igniting a heat deep in his loins. He was hard with desire, had been since lunch, when he'd tasted her in his mouth, had invited her to taste him. But now he'd reached a point where control was almost impossible. He let himself move across her body, insinuating his thighs between hers till he lay cradled against her, his erection throbbing its intent.

He didn't know if he could hold out much longer. But then he looked into Rosalie's face and read the stunned blankness there. She wanted him, but something, the furrow of surprise on her brow, gave him pause.

So he did what he'd wanted from the first—lowered his head to her breast. The fresh scent of her rose in his nostrils and her velvet-soft skin was a living caress against his chest.

He kissed her nipple, holding her tight in his arms as she almost came up off the bed in response. It was as if he'd triggered an earthquake deep inside her. The shudders echoed through her as he laved her breast. When he took her nipple in his mouth and sucked, her moans grew frantic. Her hands clenched against his skull as he tasted her sweetness, then moved to her other breast.

Restlessly her legs shifted against his and he allowed himself the luxury of pushing down against her, feeling her intimate heat against his erection, even through their clothes.

Soon.

His control was shredding, spinning away as his pulse thundered louder in his ears.

'Arik,' she whispered, 'please…'

Without thought his hand arrowed to the button on her trousers, the zip, pushing it down. He lifted himself a fraction from her as she tilted her hips and he stripped the cotton material down her thighs—enough to give him free access to the place he most wanted to be.

'Please,' she whispered again and he planted his palm between her thighs, pushing up against her sensitive core.

'Arik!' Her voice had a husky, sensual quality he loved, but when he raised his head to see her face he wondered if it was panic or delight he read on her features.

'Shh, it's all right, Rosalie. Just relax.' Her blind eyes turned to his and gradually focused. A jab of something that had the force of lightning struck right through him, making his heart leap.

Her hands slid down to cradle his neck. They were unsteady, shaking but warm and gently sensuous as they massaged his stiff muscles.

He searched her most secret place, circled and found the point he was seeking. She was hot, wet, ready.

'Arik? I don't—'

'Trust me, Rosalie.' Whatever her past sexual encounters, it was clear her experience hadn't included much pleasure.

The realisation brought anger. And a deep protectiveness, a need to ensure this was absolutely right for her.

She opened her mouth to respond as he stroked her slowly, surely, and suddenly she gasped. The light tremors that had been racing through her body became shudders. She bucked up against his hand with a force that belied her small frame. And her gaze clung to his—jade-green, brilliant and intoxicating. He could drown in that gaze, watching her come apart just for him. The thrill of it, of her body arching into his, the sound of his name on her lips again and again as she sighed out her delight, was better than anything that had gone before.

Her eyes drifted shut as the last of the vibrations subsided. His own body was on fire, desperate for release, after the heady sensations of Rosalie's climax. He slid his fingers between her legs and another aftershock racked her.

So incredibly sensual.

Gently he leaned down and took her mouth with his. Her response was instant, her lips opening to his, even though her movements were slow, languorous. He delved deep into her mouth, allowing himself the freedom he hadn't yet had with her body.

She moaned and tilted her head towards his, her fingers spreading out over his shoulders. Automatically his lower body pressed in against hers, right into the hot centre of her, and light spun behind his eyelids at the sensations of pleasure coursing through his body.

Their kiss held a different, richer quality now as she responded to his lead with a ready sultriness that urged him to deepen his caresses. The taste of her was designed to drive any man out of his senses. And the way she held him tight with her hands, the way her luscious body cushioned his, accepting and matching the insistent push of his erection against her, made his head spin.

At last he drew away, far enough that her hands broke their

hold and slid slowly, provocatively down over his chest. Her eyes were closed, her lips plump and pink with the force of their passion. A wash of colour spread across her breasts and up her cheeks, highlighting her delicate features. She breathed deeply and for a moment he was riveted by the sight of her perfect breasts, rising and falling. Hair like dawn gold flared across the silk coverlet, softer and more enticing than any man-made fabric.

Who was this woman who'd appeared out of nowhere just days ago? Who'd taken over his life? Absorbed his every waking hour and burrowed deep into his emotions?

She was a miracle.

He pushed himself up and away on his arms, then knelt to strip the last of her clothes from her. The heady scent of female arousal registered in his nostrils, inciting him to move more quickly.

It was the work of a few moments to remove her clothes, and his own, and reach for the protection he'd promised her.

Rosalie's world had tilted completely off its axis. She'd spun crazily out of control in Arik's arms as he'd brought her to a juddering, mind-blowing climax. It had been all red-hot light and heat, searing her body till she'd thought there'd be nothing left of her but ashes. Only Arik, his gaze holding hers, his body anchoring her to the spot, had brought her back to something like safety again. If it hadn't been for the link between them she felt she might have died from pure ecstasy.

His dark eyes had been the only real thing in her consciousness, other than the impossible burst of fire in her blood.

And now she felt…she squeezed her eyes shut, trying to give a name to the sense of wellbeing, of effervescent excitement that filled her, but she couldn't.

Her body was weighted, yet tingling with life. She stretched, registering for the first time the slide of the luxurious coverlet beneath her body. Her bare body. Arik had peeled away the last of her clothes just a moment ago.

Rosalie snapped open her eyes, anxious now that she couldn't feel him against her. But when she located him she swallowed hard.

He stood beside the bed, feet planted wide in a stance that was utterly masculine. He was naked, gloriously so, his dark olive skin the perfect foil for his athlete's body. Every taut muscle and powerful curve was bare for her to see. She stared, fascinated, at the fuzz of dark hair across his pectoral muscles that narrowed and disappeared as it descended. He'd make a wonderful study for an artist. Magnificent proportions, latent power and pure energy from every angle.

But she couldn't view Arik with an artist's dispassionate eye. She'd lost that objectivity.

Instead she dragged in an unsteady breath at the image of rampant male libido before her. He thrilled her. And frightened her.

He was fitting a condom. Rosalie swallowed again, her mouth suddenly dry. Surely it would break…it couldn't possibly…but it did. She felt her eyes widen.

He looked up and smiled at her, a tight, lopsided smile that nevertheless had the power to unravel some of the spiralling tension inside her.

'Rosalie,' he murmured as he took a single stride to the bed and knelt above her. 'My beautiful golden girl.' He raised her limp hand in his and kissed the palm, nipping at the fleshy part of it till a spear of heat arced straight from her hand to her womb.

How magnificent he was: so at ease in his flesh, each movement economical yet with an innate grace. The dark bronze of his body was in contrast to her own paler skin and as he lay down beside her she was fascinated by the sight of his large long-fingered hand splaying possessively across her body. Who'd have thought anything so simple could be so erotic?

Butterflies swooped in her stomach at the spreading sensation of warmth deep inside her. She felt his leg brush hers, the hair on his thigh wiry and tickling. Then he bent his head and planted a kiss at her navel.

Seismic waves spread out from the point of contact, making her shiver. The sight of his head bent over her so intimately made her conscious again of the moist heat between her legs. The empty, needy sensation.

He nuzzled her belly, planted a string of kisses across to her hip and set the butterflies dancing again inside.

She shifted uneasily, aware of a renewed urgency in the signals her body was sending to her brain.

He lifted his head and smiled, a knowing smile if ever there was one.

'You like it when I kiss you here?' He dropped his mouth once more to her waist, her stomach.

She reached out and tried to pull him up, edgy again and unsure of herself. She shouldn't feel like this again, surely.

'You don't like my kisses?' His tone was teasing but his face was set in harsh lines of desire. The flame of arousal was hot in his eyes.

She opened her mouth to answer, but something stopped her: a knot of hard, tight emotion that blocked her throat. He was so gentle, so tender. He treated her as no man ever had before. Heat glazed her eyes and she shook her head.

'Rosalie?' His tone was abrupt as he levered himself higher, the better to see her face.

For answer she wrapped her arms round his shoulders and lifted her lips to his, opening her mouth and giving herself up to the ecstasy that beckoned. Giving herself to *him*.

For a long moment he held himself rigid above her. Then, as her tongue danced against his and her hands swept in wide circles down over his back, he settled closer. She revelled in the smooth texture of his skin against her hands, and in the sensual friction of his chest hair brushing her breasts. It was…arousing. The press of his large body against hers was an exciting weight. She felt the hot, heavy throb of him between her legs and fascination mingled with trepidation.

'Rosalie,' he murmured against her mouth. 'You drive me wild with wanting.' Now their kisses were more urgent and the caress of his hands heavier, more possessive. He gripped her hips and pushed forward and she felt the hard length of him intimately against her. Instinctively she tilted her hips up towards him and he growled deep in his throat. 'You're a houri sent to bewitch me.'

He raised one hand to her breast, squeezing gently, and she let out a cry of excitement as a flaming arrow of sensation shot through her body. Above the drumming in her ears and the rocking tension in their almost-joined bodies, she heard the whisper of his deep voice in her ear. He spoke in his own language, a lyrical intonation of syllables that flowed like music around her. The words were soothing yet somehow unsettling, urging her closer as he rocked harder against her.

All she knew was him. The clean, earthy fragrance of his skin, the taste of him on her tongue, the feel of him everywhere, and still that yearning, aching sensation that couldn't be denied.

She barely noticed when he moved, hooking his arm under her thigh and lifting her leg up and over him. But she *did* register the pressure as he pushed between her legs, nudging up against her, into her.

She froze, absorbed in the sensation of him filling her.

Arik drew back a fraction. She had an impression of flashing dark eyes surveying her, then his head dipped to her breast and all capacity for coherent thought fled. His tongue was on her. His mouth. His teeth. She cried out, a muffled shout of bliss, and cradled him closer, arching her back as he wrought his magic on her body once more.

There was nothing but Arik and the dazzle of stars behind her closed eyelids.

But then, suddenly, there was more. One single, smooth, never-ending surge of movement drew him forward, impossibly filling her. She opened her eyes to see him poised above her, his face almost unrecognisable from the tension that held him so tight in its grip.

For an instant there was no movement but the rise and fall of their chests, each breathing deeply, struggling to find equilibrium.

'Lift your other leg, sweetheart.'

Slowly she complied, and then it seemed automatically he slid forward a fraction to rest deep within her. Rosalie's eyes widened.

'That's it, little one.' His kiss was a reward, a glorious, sensuous caress that made her bones melt, even as he moved again, rocking against her.

It felt…it felt…wonderful.

Rosalie slid her hands over the bunched muscles of his shoulders and down to wrap her arms around his back, to hold him close as he pushed forward again. There was something sparking between them, something that made her rise up to meet his next thrust and the next: eager, ready for him.

Their tempo increased, their bodies grew hot, slick from excitement and exertion. Rosalie felt again the welling, tingling sensation in her blood. She heard her pulse roar in her ears, heard Arik's breathing. Then his mouth closed over hers, his tongue thrusting deep even as he rocked into the centre of her being.

She tasted him, dark and rich. Scented his skin. She was part of him, his body sliding with hers, drawing her into a whirling, rushing storm of glorious commotion.

And then it came—a crashing wave of fulfilment, breaking over both of them. Desperate, she clung to Arik like a lifeline in a stormy sea. He was the one solid reality as her world shattered, bursting apart in a conflagration that shook her to her core. She had no words to express what she felt, only knew it was beyond her expectations, her hopes, even her fantasies.

And the fact that it was Arik gathering her close in strong arms that trembled with the force of their climax, holding her as if he'd never let her go, was most important of all.

How could this happen between two strangers?

It was far more surely than a union of bodies. It felt like a communion of souls.

Rosalie drew a deep shuddering breath, inhaling his heat and his musky scent.

Casual sex wasn't supposed to be this…perfect, was it?

What had she got herself into?

# CHAPTER EIGHT

'THAT sounds like fun, Amy. What are you doing with Grandma tomorrow?' Rosalie shifted her grip on the phone as her daughter began a breathless description of her planned visit to puppies in the stables and a pony who took carrots from her outstretched hand. Obviously they were far more interesting to a toddler than the grandeur of the centuries-old palace where she was staying.

Though she had been impressed with Uncle Rafiq, the tall, smiling man who swept her up in his arms and swung her round till she squealed.

Rosalie's mum was right. Amy was having a great time with her family fussing over her. Not only that, but Rafiq's small army of royal servants were spoiling her too, apparently besotted by Amy's grin and sunny temperament.

The door to Rosalie's left opened and the smile on her face slipped a little as Arik came into the room. His gaze caught hers and that gleaming dark look made her mouth dry. Like her, he wore a long, loose robe. But, far from making him look effeminate, the outfit somehow accentuated the width of his shoulders, the whipcord strength of his body, his innate masculinity.

Just a single stare from this man sent a wave of heat roaring through her. She watched him pace into the room and her palms prickled in excitement as she remembered the way he'd loved her this afternoon. The world of sensual pleasure he'd opened up for her.

Finally, half an hour ago, he'd pressed a last bone-melting kiss to her lips before leaving her, saying she'd no doubt want to telephone her daughter. Only then had she realised the afternoon had sped by as she'd lain in his arms. Shame had washed through her, that it was he rather than her who'd remembered her responsibilities. That she'd been in danger of forgetting her call to Amy.

And now, just the sight of him made it hard to concentrate on Amy's chatter.

What sort of mother was she? Surely there was something wrong with her priorities. Nothing was more important to her than her daughter.

What was happening to her?

Arik didn't approach. He gave her a slow smile that sent liquid heat spilling down her spine. Then he disappeared through the door to the huge bathroom. It was a relief when he was out of sight and that sensual connection was severed.

An instant later she heard the sound of running water. She blinked, trying to bring her mind back to her call.

'I have to go now, Mummy. G'anma says it's time to hang up.'

'All right, sweetheart. You be a good girl for Grandma and Auntie Belle and I'll see you soon.'

'I will, Mummy. Bye, bye.'

'Bye, darling.'

Slowly Rosalie switched off the phone and put it beside the huge bed. Another sign of Arik's generosity, or more likely his enormous wealth. He didn't know Amy was actually in Q'aroum rather than at home in Australia. He would have assumed when he'd offered Rosalie the use of the phone that she'd be making an international call.

It only highlighted the difference between Arik's world and

her life of stretching to make ends meet. Despite persistent offers from Belle, Rosalie had been so determined to stand on her own two feet she'd accepted little financial help. The holiday to Q'aroum was an exception.

'You didn't need to end your call just yet.' Arik's deep voice interrupted her reverie and she looked up to find him framed by the doorway, watching her.

The look in his eyes made her shiver. Or perhaps it was remembered delight. She'd never experienced that incandescent burst of joy, that absolute sense of oneness with another person in her life. Arik had been all her fantasies rolled into one—strong, passionate and indescribably gentle. She felt as if she'd unwittingly given up part of herself to him through the act of making love. At the time it had seemed right—more than that, it had seemed perfect. Now the idea created a niggle of unease deep inside her.

She was in danger of getting in too deep. It was one thing to think in terms of a holiday fling with a gorgeous man: a safe way to experience passion and then move on, back to her ordinary life, her curiosity satisfied.

But this was something else altogether. It was as if an unseen link stretched between them. Even now she felt it tightening, tugging at her as he strode over to the bed.

She looked up into his black eyes and knew it was an unwinnable battle, trying to remain unmoved by him. He was in her blood, in her very bones. Somehow she'd absorbed him into herself. She had an overwhelming fear that now she'd never be the same again. Never be whole without him.

'Your daughter is well?' He smiled down at her and the melting rush of desire in the pit of her stomach commenced again.

'She's having a ball.' Rosalie ignored the breathless quality of her voice, swallowing hard at the excitement humming through her, just being close to him again. 'She's with her aunt and uncle and my mother. I suspect she's being spoiled rotten.'

Arik's grin was a flash of white in his dark face. 'That's as it should be. Every child deserves to be spoiled a little by their family. And it will take her mind off being away from you.'

Rosalie tilted her head, registering his words. Most men she knew wouldn't consider it from that angle. They weren't so sympathetic to the needs of others, would barely give a thought to what a little child needed.

But then, she'd never met a man like Arik before. So utterly, devastatingly male but compassionate too.

'You speak as if you've got some insight into it,' she said, suddenly curious to know more about him. In so many ways she knew him intimately: his character, his passion, his body. But she knew next to nothing about his life.

He shrugged. 'I'm an only child but I have a large, loving extended family. My childhood was spent learning discipline and responsibility from my father, and being indulged by almost everyone else. We Q'aroumis are especially fond of children, you know.'

'And your mother?'

'Ah, my mother is a woman of strong passions.' His dark eyes flashed. 'It was she who taught me to follow my heart. She believes that you can achieve whatever you set your heart on, so long as you never give up.'

Arik leaned close, his intense expression making her feel suddenly vulnerable. Something akin to apprehension skittered through her as she looked up, up at him. The stark planes and angles of his face were more pronounced in the late afternoon light, emphasising his strength and the slightly exotic cast of his features.

*He's a stranger*, whispered a voice in her head. *A man you barely know, and yet you let him—*

No! She knew Arik in the ways that counted. Knew his integrity, his caring. She knew exactly where she stood with him. They'd made a bargain. She was perfectly safe.

And yet…when he stared at her like that it made her wonder.

'Come.' He stepped forward and slid his hands beneath her, hauling her up into his arms. Automatically she clung to him, her hands linking round his neck. Her heart thudded to a quickening beat, just being in contact with him again. She revelled in the now familiar heat of his body against hers.

'Where are we going?'

His black gaze held hers in a look that made the blood rush to her face and anticipation sizzle in the pit of her stomach.

'Enough talking for now, Rosalie.' He shouldered his way through the open door and into the enormous bathroom.

Her eyes widened as she took in the octagonal room. On four sides huge windows gave out on to the spectacular cliff top view. And in the centre, right below the domed gilt ceiling, was the largest bath she'd ever seen. It was sunk into the floor, half filled with steamy water and bubbles. Sandalwood scented the air and something else—some fragrance that was heavy and lush.

Her racing heartbeat slowed to a lazy expectant beat. Then he was putting her down, letting her slide, inch by tantalising inch, down his body. Like her he was naked beneath the robe. And somehow the fact that they were both fully covered only enhanced the sensuality of the experience. The slide of hot silk against her flesh. The press of his hard body, ridged with muscle and flagrantly aroused, yet covered in the finest cotton, was even more erotic than seeing him naked.

Rosalie's mouth was dry as she found her footing. Her hands were linked around his neck. She tightened her hold, drawing his head closer while she rose on tiptoe.

'No.' He shook his head. 'Not yet.'

Her expression must have revealed her disappointment for he lifted one hand to her mouth, pressed his thumb against her bottom lip till she opened for him, and she tasted him, warm and salty on her tongue. Heat burst in the pit of her belly and down her legs, till she trembled where she stood.

'Soon,' he promised. Then, with one swift movement, he bent and gathered the silken skirts of her gown in his hands, skimming the fabric up her legs. Up and up till she felt the whisper-soft afternoon breeze on her thighs, her stomach, her breasts.

She watched the play of muscles in his upper arms as he flung the gossamer-thin robe to the floor.

Now his hands brushed against her, feathering up her legs, over her buttocks, her hips, her waist, to her breasts, heavy with the weight of desire. Moist heat pooled between her legs as she looked deep into his eyes. They were glazed with an excitement that matched her own.

Cotton bunched in her fingers. She lifted the weight of his robe, scrabbling a little as the fabric shifted. Underneath the material she felt tantalising traces of his body—the heavy weight of his muscled thigh as she bent low, the angle of his hip-bone and the ridged muscles of his abdomen. There was a hiss of breath as she shoved the robe higher, her hand sliding across his chest. Then he bent his head, allowed her to draw the garment off him and toss it away.

A weight settled on her chest, pressing down, making it hard to breathe as she skimmed his body with her gaze.

He was magnificent.

'If you look at me like that, this will be over before it's begun.'

She slanted a look up at his face. He seemed to be in pain, so great was the tension there. Had she done that to him? Her presence? Her body? It was a heady thought.

'Get in the bath, Rosalie, and I'll join you in a moment.' His voice was soft, a whisper. But he'd lost his smooth tones. Now his words were rough, as if something grated deep inside him. The sound was a primal message of barely restrained hunger that fed her excitement.

Quickly she turned and stepped into the deep bath, luxuriating in the feel of warm water sliding against her bare skin. In the knowledge that Arik would be with her soon.

He almost groaned aloud as he watched her descend into the foam. That peach-ripe *derrière*, the long, long legs, the indentation of her waist, so small he could almost span it with his hands. He fumbled, rolling on the condom. His whole body was shaking, throbbing with the force of his desire.

She turned, her eyes wide as she watched him lower himself into the bath, reminding him that, for all her enthusiasm and her natural sensuality, Rosalie was a woman of little experience.

The shock on her face as they'd become one, the wonder in her expression as she'd scaled the heights of passion, the hesitant way she'd embraced him at first...it had almost been like making love to a virgin.

The experience had been new to him. Far too quickly he'd become hooked by the thrill of surprising her, of teaching her about her body's own sweet secrets. And when she'd reciprocated, caressing him, moving with him, it had been as if together they'd ignited dynamite. The explosive force of their joint climax had deserved a Richter scale warning.

He was a man who enjoyed women. Enjoyed sex. He was a man of some experience. But nothing, ever, had matched the sheer ecstasy of making love to Rosalie Winters.

He'd wanted her again almost immediately. Even now he couldn't say how he'd managed to tear himself away long enough for her to recover and to phone home.

It would be the challenge of a lifetime to take this slow. She was temptation personified. She looked at him with those huge green eyes, her lips pouted and pink, her nipples teasing him, just peeping up through the bubbles when she moved. Involuntarily he throbbed in response, just at the sight of her.

He turned and wrenched off the taps, wishing he could

turn off his libido, or at least slow it down long enough to wrest control.

'Come here, Rosalie.' He lifted a hand in invitation and immediately she slid along the seat that edged the deep bath. Her hand rested in his and he drew her closer. He felt her hip beside his and immediately turned to claim her, one hand at her neck, as he slanted his mouth over hers, the other wrapping round her waist.

She was unique. He'd only known the taste of her for a few days and yet he craved it more than food or drink. She tilted her head back, allowing him better access to her mouth, and he took it, delving deeply, possessively, as he pressed her slippery form against his. He thrust a thigh between hers and felt the little jitter of reaction race through her body.

He smiled against her mouth. She was so ready.

When he cupped her breast in his palm she pushed against his hand, a sound like a hungry purr rolling deep in her throat. She slid against him, her hips circling, and he let his weight rest against her.

If he wanted he could take her now. With one swift movement he could possess her. Fierce heat pumped in his bloodstream at the thought of taking her hard and fast right now. Completion would be only seconds away.

But he held back. He wanted to give her more than a quick, hard coupling. And to do that he needed to hold out against the barbaric impulse to ravish. Somehow he had to find finesse. He needed to forget his own needs and—

Lightning struck to his heart as her small hand closed round him. He shuddered, surging forward into her intimate caress, unable to temper his hungry response. His tongue probed her mouth as he pushed against her hand, exulting in the sensation even as he recognised it wasn't enough.

'Don't!' The word was a low growl as he gripped her shoulders and leaned back. 'Don't touch me.'

'You don't like it?' There was no teasing lilt to her voice and her eyes were serious. Something hard knotted tight in his chest at the sight of her doubt, the way she bit down on her lush bottom lip as if afraid she'd done the wrong thing.

She genuinely didn't know what she did to him!

Breathing raggedly, Arik cupped her chin in his palm and felt her racing pulse flutter beneath her chin. He looked deep into her eyes, drawn by her honesty, registering her confusion.

'I love the feel of your hand on me, Rosalie. Too much.'

Her mouth opened in a delicious pout of surprise and Arik cursed the need for restraint. He dragged in an unsteady breath as desire warred with caution. 'That's the problem. That's why you have to stop.'

Instantly her hold on him tightened and another searing jolt of heat surged through him. He thrust against her, helpless to resist.

He drew in deep, scouring lungfuls of air and sought for strength. Strength to resist her.

His hand trembled as he gripped her wrist and drew her hand away, sliding his fingers through hers and holding her hand between them. With his other hand he reached down to cup her breast, squeezing gently till she sighed her pleasure. She moved restlessly against him, her body responding sinuously to his caresses. He took her mouth again and arrowed his hand down to the tender place between her thighs, exploring, probing, till she gasped and bucked into his touch.

'No!' She writhed against him, tore her hand from his grip. She planted her hands on his chest, pushing hard. 'No, Arik. Please.'

He looked down into her flushed face and knew a great tenderness for this remarkable woman. Whatever she wanted he'd give her.

'It's you I need,' she gasped. 'Please.'

How could he resist such an appeal? She shook against

him, her soft body against his iron-hard frame an invitation to pleasure. The knowledge of her desire was the strongest seduction of all.

With one sure movement he settled back on the tiled seat and swung her up till she straddled him, kneeling on the wide underwater bench. Next time, he promised himself. Next time he'd take it more slowly, tease her and tempt her and draw out each pleasure with infinite patience till she swooned with delight. Next time he'd be strong.

'Come down,' he whispered, his voice hoarse and unsteady as he cupped her breasts and leaned forward to draw her nipple into his mouth. The hiss of her indrawn breath was sweet, almost as sweet as the sensation of her velvety heat teasing his erection.

He sucked harder, tightening his hold, hearing her gasp. And then slowly, so incredibly slowly, she shifted, bearing down, allowing him the entry he craved.

It was death by degrees, ecstasy in such slow motion it must surely kill him. He slid his hands down to her waist, clamping hard and drawing her down lower, further till at last they were one.

Paradise.

He looked into her eyes and was lost. How could any woman be both seductress and innocent? She had the body, the erotic instincts of a wanton and yet she seemed so untutored, almost amazed at the sensations she aroused. He wanted to ravish her and yet protect her. Take her with the full force of the merciless need she awoke in him, and at the same time cherish her with gentle words and soothing caresses.

Then she moved, tilted her hips experimentally, and cogent thought fled. Arik let his hands slide down to the swell of her hips as he pushed up against her. Saw her eyes widen as a wave of pleasure hit them both.

'Arik? I...'

Her voice dwindled as the ripples of pleasure began deep

inside her. So soon, so strong that they tugged at him, loosening his control, making his hands slip as he moved against her, instinctively adopting the rhythm that they both needed. She moved with him and there was magic in their tempo, in the hungry slide of flesh into flesh, in the matched drum beat of their hearts pounding as one.

He'd never seen anything more magnificent than the blaze of ecstasy in her jade-bright eyes.

Completion came upon them hard and fast, obliterating everything in a rush of ecstasy so brilliant, so fantastic, that it should be impossible. It was endless, like the sound of her soft mews of excitement, like the roaring locomotive rush of blood in his ears, like his desire for her—building and never diminishing.

When at last it was over she slumped, boneless, against him, his arms wrapped possessively around her. His body was weak in the aftermath of a force stronger than anything he'd known and only one thought circled in his numbed brain. *Next time*. Next time he'd take it slowly. Next time he wouldn't give in to pleasure so fast. Next time he'd love her as she deserved to be loved…

Dawn light cast an amber-pink glow across the room, the wide bed, the man lying beside her, one arm stretched out to curve round her waist, holding her close, even in sleep.

All through the evening and the long night she and Arik had been together: touching, caressing. Even when she slept she'd merely dozed in his arms and had woken to find him alert and watching her, the heat of his gaze immediately firing her blood. She'd been wanton, eager and ready for his loving, an ever-willing pupil as he'd taught her about physical desire, and about herself.

She'd revelled in his tempered strength, his tenderness and patience.

She stared into his beautiful face, traced the planes of his jaw, the high angles of his cheekbones, the strong shape of his nose, the sensual line of his lips. Something tumbled over in her stomach as she remembered those lips on her body, exquisitely sensitive, roughly demanding, making her want things, do things, she'd never before dreamed of.

Her gaze drifted to the wide spread of his shoulders, his deep chest, where she'd nuzzled, feeling safe as never before in his strong embrace.

Again that sensation of heat churned deep inside her. But this time it didn't presage sexual desire, the urgent need for completion that Arik had taught her so much about. This was deeper, more disturbing.

Rosalie swallowed down hard on the constriction in her throat as she summoned the strength to face reality after a night so wonderful it rivalled fantasy.

She'd always known she wasn't the type to enjoy a casual affair. That had never been her style. And the traumatic events over three years ago had only increased her caution.

Yet she'd succumbed to Arik's seduction with barely a protest. She couldn't claim she'd been swept away in the heat of the moment. No, despite the force of her suddenly awakened physical longings, she'd made a conscious decision to accept what Arik offered. She'd wanted him, wanted the simmering passion that flared between them every time they were close. She'd wanted to satisfy her curiosity, learn about desire and sex and passion. She'd told herself that with Arik she was safe. He wouldn't take more than she wanted to give. He would treat her well.

And when it was over she could walk away, back to her real life, secure in the knowledge that it had been only a holiday affair, a moment's snatched pleasure in a life focused on rebuilding her future and raising her daughter. Nothing would change.

*But it had.*

She'd deceived herself.

Rosalie squeezed her eyes shut, breathing deep as she sought for strength. The warm, musky scent of his skin teased her, the evocative scent of sex. She opened her eyes to his face, relaxed in sleep yet so strong and now so dear. She'd been deliberately blind to the consequences as she'd given herself to him. Blind to the warning signals, ignoring danger with a single-minded determination to live for the moment.

Now she had to pay the price.

The circling sensation in her stomach turned to a twist of pain as she stared at him, memorising his unique features.

She wanted to lift her hand and stroke his face, feel the stubble darkening his jaw, tease his mouth with her own, nestle against the hard, warm wall of his chest where the fuzz of black hair would tease her breasts into tingling expectation of his loving.

But she daredn't. She understood her weakness now. That was one thing Arik had taught her well. She knew that once he took her in his arms she'd be lost. She'd succumb to the magic of his body against hers, the craving for him that even now was unabated. She'd never get away, not until he was ready to call a halt.

And by that time she'd be even deeper in his thrall. It didn't bear thinking about.

The truth was that Arik was far more to her than a casual partner. There was nothing casual about what she felt for him. There never had been. Instinctively she'd known it but she'd shunned the truth, hiding behind the facile argument that it was a short-term romance, easily ended.

Heat prickled at the back of her eyes as she looked for the last time at his face, imprinting it on her memory.

Better to go now. End this affair before he realised how she felt. She didn't think she could face his pity.

After all, their time was up, wasn't it? She'd finished her artwork yesterday. Had it only been then? Vaguely she remembered the sense of satisfaction, of pleasure at her achievement. Technically her agreement with Arik was over.

Did she have the strength to fight her own desperate longing and do what must be done?

# CHAPTER NINE

'NO, SIR. I've double-checked. We've had no Rosalie Winters staying with us. No Australians at all in the last month.'

'All right, thank you for checking.' Arik severed the connection and drew in a deep breath.

*Think, man.* She wasn't at either of the beachfront hotels or the smaller guest houses. But she couldn't have vanished into thin air. Where could she have been staying?

His fist clenched more tightly on the crumpled paper. The rustling sound fuelled his anger.

What had she thought she was doing, leaving him such a note? Stilted phrases swirled in his head, indelibly printed there.

*It's been wonderful…*

*Better if we didn't see each other again…*

And finally, devastatingly: *Thank you.*

Thank you! As if he'd done her some small courtesy, a trifling favour that required acknowledgement.

His pulse throbbed furiously and his jaw gritted more tightly at the audacity of the woman's actions.

As if he was some casual acquaintance to be fobbed off with polite thanks! Or, worse, as if he'd served his purpose and could now be dismissed, left behind like some cheap souvenir she'd decided not to buy.

As if they hadn't been lovers. Lovers in a way he'd never

been with any other woman. Each moment with her had been so intense, so addictively exciting. He'd even learned to enjoy her abstracted silence as she'd focused on her painting rather than him. He'd delighted in her pleasure, had been moved by her appreciation of his country and enjoyed her quick wit almost as much as he'd adored her body.

They'd shared the best sex he'd ever experienced and he refused to be cheated of more.

How dared she leave him like that? No explanation. No possible reason to run from him like a thief in the night.

That was what she'd done—scurried away when he'd finally fallen asleep, as if she couldn't bring herself to face him. As if she were *ashamed* of the pleasure they'd found together, of the intimacy that had stunned him with its rare potency.

It was for him to feel shame that he'd let their liaison mean so much. He'd allowed Rosalie Winters to get under his skin in a way no woman ever had. With her apparent innocence, her sweet seductiveness, she'd been stringing him along all the time, using *him* and then running away. No doubt she was eager to share the story of her holiday romance with her friends.

Arik frowned. No, despite his fury, he couldn't believe that of her. She was no manipulator.

But then, what had gone wrong? Why her sudden flight?

He spun on his foot and strode out on to the balcony, staring down for the hundredth time at the beach below, unmarked by footprints since the last high tide. No sign of her familiar figure returning around the point.

Something hard and tight jammed up high in his ribs. A pain, an ache. A rough, burning sensation that made him want to reach out and strike something.

He would not allow it. Of course their relationship had to end at some point. He'd always known it.

*But not yet.*

*Not now.*

*Not till he was ready.*

An afternoon and a night with Rosalie in his arms had merely whetted his appetite for her, not sated it. Whatever bizarre notion she had about leaving, he'd persuade her out of it. Even if it meant postponing his return to work for a week or two—for long enough to have his fill of her.

He punched out the number for the local airport on his cellphone, then leaned on the parapet while he spoke to one of the administrators.

Within a few minutes he'd confirmed that Rosalie had taken a flight to the Q'aroumi capital within the last hour. She must have broken the land speed record to get there in time.

There were no more flights to the main island today but that was no problem; he could use his helicopter. And, besides, he knew there were no connecting international flights to Australia for a couple of days. Plenty of time to locate her and persuade her to return. It even fitted his schedule. He was due in the capital himself tomorrow afternoon for an official engagement.

Arik's mouth curved in a tight smile. When he found Rosalie Winters she'd soon beg for his lovemaking. He'd make sure of that. No more holding back. The time for caution had passed. Rosalie would feel the full, unfettered force of his passion. It would be a simple thing to convince her she'd made a mistake. After all, she was so satisfyingly eager for his touch.

He'd take his pleasure with her till the bright, flaming need burned itself out, as it inevitably would.

Then, only then, would he agree to end their affair.

He swung round and paced back into his room. First he'd find out which hotel she'd booked into and then he'd visit his errant lover.

His lips curved into a slow smile. He looked forward to persuading her to stay.

* * *

A day later Arik stared across the myriad of people filling the audience chamber in Q'aroum's royal palace. He felt as if an enormous unseen weight had slammed straight into his solar plexus. The air slid out of his lungs in a whoosh of shock. He could barely believe his eyes.

No wonder he'd found no trace of Rosalie at any of the hotels. Nor at the guest houses or private *pensions* that flourished in the city.

He hadn't understood how she'd vanished without a trace. Until now. Until he'd looked across the massive room to the royal family.

There were his cousin Rafiq and his cousin's wife, Belle, holding their son, Adham. The first birthday of the heir to Q'aroum's throne was the reason for this royal reception. Behind Rafiq and Belle stood an older woman in western dress who could only be Belle's mother. The family resemblance between the two women was strong. Even with her greying hair she was handsome, her face full of character.

And by her side, partly hidden from view, was another younger woman. The trousers and long-sleeved tunic she wore covered her figure but couldn't conceal it. Not when the jade silk skimmed voluptuous breasts, revealed a neat waist as she turned to talk to the man beside her. Not when Arik already knew every centimetre of that siren's body. Not when the feel of it, the scent of it, the taste of it, were imprinted on his brain.

*Rosalie.*

Her name echoed in his stunned brain as he viewed the scene.

There was no mistake. She had to be Belle's sister. Just look at the shape of those eyes, that mouth, that neat determined chin. Mirror images they weren't, but there was enough similarity to put the connection beyond doubt.

His lover was Rafiq's sister-in-law.

Arik sucked in a breath that shuddered through his oxygen-starved chest as he absorbed the implications.

She was related to royalty. More than that—she was, by marriage, a member of his own extended family. Rafiq, though by blood no closer than a second cousin, was like a brother to him. They'd grown up together, shared a bond that had strengthened as they'd weathered the early loss of parents: Rafiq's parents in a 'copter smash and Arik's father from sudden illness.

If he'd known who Rosalie was from the start he'd have put all thought of an affair from his mind. Not because he'd have wanted to, but because he would have had no choice. He was bound by familial ties, by custom, by the merest common courtesy, much less the respect he felt for Rafiq, not to seduce her into his bed.

Her connections made her eminently unsuitable for a short-term sexual liaison, no matter how willing she was.

Pain twisted deep in his chest as he remembered to breathe again. He dragged in more air.

There was no going back. What was done was done. His body already knew hers, knew and craved its sweet softness. And yet any chance of resuming their liaison had just been destroyed by the knowledge of her true identity.

Arik clenched his fists at his sides, feeling the burning need, the ravening hunger, still hot in his blood. He could have howled his frustration aloud, staring across the room at the woman who unquestionably he couldn't have.

By any calculation she was out of bounds.

The light caught her bright blonde hair as she tipped her face up and smiled at something Rafiq said. Instantly, unreasonably, Arik's blood boiled, searing his veins with futile jealousy. That she should share that smile, even that minor intimacy, with any man other than himself, fed his frustration.

He wanted her. More—he *craved* her. Even now, just

watching her across the thronged room, his body hummed its need, his groin tightening in sexual anticipation of the woman he'd already claimed as his own.

He hadn't rested since she'd left his bed. Instead he'd been haunted by the memory of her seductive body, her bright eyes, her gentle laugh and her sharp mind.

And now to discover she was untouchable…

It was more than flesh and blood could bear.

Was that why she'd kept her identity a secret? To string him along?

He shook his head, trying to clear it. No, Rosalie wasn't that calculating. Whatever the reason for her reticence, he was sure it wasn't that.

Across the room the crowd shifted, revealing another golden head in the group. The fluffy curls belonged to a little girl with the face of an angel and her mother's wide smile. Amy.

Arik stared, conscious of a queer hollow sensation in his chest as he watched Rosalie bend down to talk to her daughter. Something squeezed hard inside him as he watched the pair. The love between them was obvious, bright as day.

Suddenly, unbelievably, he felt an arrow of piercing discomfort, watching the intimacy between them. He breathed deep, deliberately unclenching his tight fists and spreading his fingers. He couldn't be jealous of her relationship with her daughter. That would be bizarre.

And yet…strong emotion gripped him tight around the heart as he watched the two of them and knew he was forever denied the intimacy he wanted with this woman. The intimacy he'd only just discovered and now yearned for with an intensity that threatened to unman him.

'Her name's Rosalie,' a female voice said beside him.

Startled, Arik swung round, silently cursing the possibility that his thoughts had been revealed on his face as he'd stood brooding.

But the woman hadn't spoken to him. She'd addressed her comment to another middle aged woman with a tight, sour face. The pair stood a little to his right, their heads bent together as they surveyed the crowd.

'Pretty enough, like her sister,' responded the other woman. 'But pretty is as pretty does, I always say. And there's more to that one than meets the eye.'

'Really?' The first woman lowered her voice. 'What have you heard?'

Arik held his breath. He'd been so discreet, at least in public, that no one should guess his private interest in Rosalie. And his staff were utterly loyal and discreet. They wouldn't have spread gossip about her. But had something leaked out? Something that might hurt her?

'Well, you see her little daughter? She doesn't have a father. He's not dead and there was no divorce. In fact—' the woman tilted her head closer to her friend '—I've heard that she refuses to name the father. If you ask me, that's just an excuse. She probably *can't* name the father. You know how young women are these days.'

'Unfortunately there don't seem to be enough fine, upstanding older women to provide an example to them.' The words were out of Arik's mouth even as he turned to confront the speaker.

He watched two pairs of eyes grow round, two mouths gape as the women looked up at him. Some savage inner self wished they were men, young and fit, so he could find a physical outlet for the blood-red rage that marred his vision and pumped in his arteries. It would take only the slightest provocation to tempt him to violence.

Slowly he drew breath, tempered his aggressive response.

'Surely it's Q'aroumi custom to be hospitable to newcomers?' he asked, arching a brow. 'It's a sad state of affairs when a stranger is subjected to malicious gossip by those who should know better. I wonder how our host would react if he heard such rumours spread under his own roof?'

Their reaction would have been comical if their offence weren't so great. He heard their apologies, their excuses, watched the embarrassment and chagrin on their faces as they scuttled away. But he felt no satisfaction.

Instead he wanted to take something in his bare hands and break it. Smash it. Pulverise it.

He raged at this impossible situation. He wanted Rosalie. He wanted her in his bed again but now he recognised he needed so much more. Above all he wanted to protect her, even from the harm he might do to her reputation among the more strait-laced of his people.

He set his jaw and swung round to face the royal party. His eyes narrowed.

It was time he paid his respects to his hosts.

Rosalie was talking to Amy when she heard him.

For a moment she thought she imagined it. The low liquid sound of his voice that brushed across her skin and sent a quiver of longing through her. It had to be a hallucination, a trick of her subconscious, to think Arik was here.

She bit down hard on her lip, summoning the resolve she'd tested to the limits in the last thirty-six hours.

Was it that long since she'd left him? The dull, persistent ache deep in her chest told her it was all that and more.

Then she heard him again. *Arik!*

She swung round, hampered by her crouching position, and almost collapsed in a heap.

It was him. Here. Only a couple of metres away.

He stood talking to Rafiq and Belle and, from the sound of it, they were old friends. Why hadn't she thought of that? As leader of his tribe, he was an important figure in Q'aroum. He was probably on the central government council that Rafiq had mentioned. And the way Arik and her brother-in-law were greeting each other, it was clear their relationship was more than one of formal protocol. There was genuine affection in their voices.

Rosalie's head spun as she tried to think through the implications. Had he seen her? Did he know who she was? And how was she going to face him again and pretend polite interest when the mere sound of his voice smashed straight through her defences? Already the warm liquid spill of desire swirled low in her body in eager anticipation of his touch.

Helplessly she stared at him. From this level she had an excellent view of his long, soft leather boots, hand-stitched and supple. Loose trousers in pristine white that just hinted at the strength of those powerful thighs beneath. A wide sash embroidered in reds and gold in place of a belt and, in it, the jewelled sheath and haft of a ceremonial knife. Shirt of finest linen, high-necked and adorned with the tiniest hint of gold stitching. A long pale cloak, flung back over his shoulders. A head scarf of purest white, bound in gold, that only served to emphasise the magnificent bronze of his strong neck and aristocratic face.

It was Arik, but Arik as she'd never seen him. Arik the sheikh, the nobleman. The stranger.

Realising her vulnerable position down on the floor, Rosalie stumbled to her feet, pulling Amy into her arms.

Her heart thudded out of control as, for an instant, she contemplated fleeing the room. Escaping before he saw her. But that was impossible. Already Belle was introducing him to their mother. Any minute now…

'And this is my sister, Rosalie. And her daughter, Amy.'

Eyes dark as the velvet night sky pinioned her. They blazed with an inner fire that somehow leapt across the intervening space and into her bloodstream. Heat scorched through her body, the familiar burn of desire.

But it wasn't just physical wanting that she read in his expression. She'd seen that and welcomed it before. This was something else. Something even stronger. More dangerous.

'Rosalie?' There was concern in Belle's voice but Rosalie couldn't drag her gaze away from the man who stared down at her with such intensity.

She'd opened her mouth, searching for the non-committal, polite words suitable for the occasion, when Arik spoke.

'Hello, Rosalie.' Just that. But in such a tone, his voice laced with dark honey, that there could be no doubt in anyone's mind that they'd met before.

In her peripheral vision Rosalie saw Belle shift suddenly. Beside her Rafiq stood, unmoving, watching.

And all the while Rosalie sought her voice, spellbound as much by the sight and sound of her lover as by the need that pulsed even now deep inside her.

'I didn't expect to see you here.' Was that anger in Arik's voice? She'd focused so much on her own need for flight that she'd barely considered how angry he might be at her sudden departure.

If she'd been stronger she'd have stayed and told him of her decision to leave. No doubt then he'd have shrugged and accepted her decision. After all, he was only interested in a short-term fling. It must be pique at her sudden departure that made his jaw clench so tight, his nostrils flare.

'Hello, Arik.' Her voice sounded rusty. She swallowed hard and took refuge from his searing eyes by turning to her daughter. Her arms tightened protectively around her.

'Amy, this is Arik.'

Her daughter's eyes were wide as she looked up into the dark face above them. For a long moment she considered him and then her face split into a wide sunny grin.

'Hello.'

'Hello, Amy. It's nice to meet you. I've heard lots about you.'

Rosalie turned back to see him smiling at her daughter. Gone from his expression was the heat, the hardness. He looked almost…gentle.

Something shifted inside her as she stared up at the man who meant so much to her, watching him bestow his winning smile on her little girl.

For a single insane instant Rosalie found herself wishing things were different…wishing for the impossible.

'You know each other?' Belle stepped forward and Rosalie saw the curiosity on her sister's face. That expression told her she wasn't going to escape without a detailed explanation. She'd better have her story ready for when they were in private.

'Yes.' Rosalie cleared her throat. 'We met on the beach one morning just before Mum and Amy flew over here to join you.'

'Just a single meeting?' Was that disappointment in her sister's voice or disbelief?

Rosalie slanted a look up at Arik but there was no help to be had there. His lips were closed in a firm line.

'No. More than that. I spent a couple of mornings painting a beach scene and Arik helped me. I mean—'

'Rosalie saw my horses swimming and wanted one in the scene she was painting. It was my pleasure to agree.'

'So you had Ahmed bring the horses down for Rosalie to paint?' Rafiq spoke for the first time, his voice cool.

Arik looked down into her face, his expression bland, his eyes blazing, and Rosalie wondered that she didn't catch fire from the heat he radiated. Could no one else see that incendiary spark in his gaze?

'No.' He shook his head slowly. 'I was at a loose end, unable to return to my normal routine. I took the horses to the beach myself for Rosalie to paint.'

He turned abruptly to meet Rafiq's gaze. There was a challenge in his expression and in the taut line of his jaw. He didn't move but suddenly Arik looked bigger, broader, the set of his shoulders almost confrontational.

Something passed between the two men in that silent moment. As if they held a wordless communication shared by no one else.

Then Arik's features relaxed and Rafiq smiled. He clapped a hand to Arik's shoulder. 'You're so proud of those horses of yours. Anyone would think they rivalled the ones in my own stable.'

'It's a good thing for you, cousin, that I have the good manners not to argue with my host. I will merely observe that it's clearly too long since you rode one of my horses.'

'Cousin?' Rosalie breathed out the word.

'Rafiq and Arik are related,' Belle answered, still watching her closely. 'I forget the specific details but they're family, as you can see.'

Rafiq was already suggesting a horse race to settle the issue of which were the better horses. But his smile was wide and his expression easy as he bantered with Arik.

'Yes. I see,' Rosalie whispered.

This situation was impossible. Bad enough to be pining for a man she couldn't have. To realise she'd made the biggest mistake of her life in succumbing to the charm of the one man who embodied all her secret fantasies. But to be forced to face him in the intimacy of her over-protective family circle, where everyone was obsessed with her welfare… It was unthinkable.

She breathed deep against the sudden sensation of the walls closing in around her. Trapping her. The conversation morphed into a low background buzz and a chill nibbled at her spine.

She hadn't felt this sudden sense of unreasoning panic in so long. Had hoped it was a thing of the past, like the worst of the nightmares.

'Rosalie. Are you all right?'

Arik's voice broke across her consciousness, shattering

her sense of isolation. Gratefully she looked up at him. His intent, encouraging look warmed her from the inside out. Her heart thudded painfully and life pulsed back into her chest. Automatically she shifted Amy up higher on her hip.

'Yes. I'm okay.'

'But you've been running around after Amy since dawn,' her mother said from beside her. 'It's time you had a rest.' She reached out her arms. 'Here, Amy, come and spend some time with Grandma.'

Reluctantly Rosalie let her daughter go. Without Amy held close in her arms she felt vulnerable, far too exposed to Arik's attention.

But she needn't have worried. Seconds later she was surrounded by animated discussions. Arik and her brother-in-law amicably disputed the rival claims of their stables. Her mother and Belle checked on little Adham, the birthday boy, fast asleep in an ornate gilded cot. They debated how long before he woke and whether Belle could slip him away for a quiet feed. Amy suggested they offer him ice cream and peaches, her current favourite foods.

Rosalie listened to their voices and the amorphous noise rising from the wider crowd and longed to be alone with her thoughts.

She lasted through another hour of introductions and light chat, of official speeches in honour of Adham and of watching Amy while she played with some new found friends. Then, finally, Rosalie noticed people beginning to say their goodbyes. She could leave now without feeling she was breaking up the special occasion.

With a murmured word to her mother, she led Amy away and down the labyrinthine passages of the old palace. Her daughter was almost out on her feet with excitement and lack of her usual daytime nap, so getting her ready for bed took far less time than usual.

Soon Amy was sleeping soundly and Rosalie looked out at the darkening night sky. Strangely, she felt lonelier than she had in years, even standing here, listening to her daughter's soft breathing.

*He'd* done this to her. *Arik.*

He'd unsettled her, made her yearn for so much that she couldn't have, especially from him.

That sense of claustrophobia haunted her. She wanted to be outside where she could breathe deeply and banish the remains of those old haunting fears.

Five minutes later she stood on an ancient stone balcony jutting out from the citadel bastion, looking out over the sea. A glow of sunset pink rimmed the horizon as the sky darkened from azure to indigo.

Rosalie sighed her relief. She'd found this quiet spot on her first visit. Something about the view and the solitude always invigorated her, helped her to think.

What would she do if Arik decided to stay and spend time with his cousin? She wasn't due to leave Q'aroum for several weeks and she'd arouse suspicion and worry her family if she left early. Yet she didn't think she could manage to treat him as a polite, amiable acquaintance. Not while her body and her soul burned for so much more.

But what alternative did she have?

She was leaning out over the parapet, her hands planted on the stonework, when something made her stiffen.

The sound of the massive old door dragging shut behind her.

'Hello, Rosalie,' said the low, sultry voice that haunted her dreams. 'I thought I might find you here.'

# CHAPTER TEN

ROSALIE spun round to face him and he realised with despair that she looked more gorgeous than ever. Her tunic top was wrinkled on one side where Amy had clung and her hair was rumpled, as if tiny fingers had played with those rose-gold strands. Her eyes were huge, her lips parted.

Arik liked her this way—slightly mussed. As if she'd come straight from his bed. Or was just going there.

Muscles spasmed tight in his belly and groin at the thought. The inevitability of his reaction only fuelled his anger. He crossed his arms over his chest and waited. He was looking forward to hearing her explanation.

'I wasn't expecting to see you here.' Her voice was light and breathless, as it had been back in the audience chamber. No wonder her family had watched them closely. She'd sounded so obviously like a woman hiding secrets.

'Weren't you?' He stared down at her. 'You expected me to remain at home, satisfied with that farcical note you left me?' Fury bubbled up inside him as he remembered the trite little missive. She hadn't even thought him worthy of a face-to-face explanation!

She shook her head. 'I didn't know you were coming to the reception.'

'If you'd been honest with me, Rosalie, I'd have told you

my plans. I had no idea you were part of Rafiq's family or that you'd be here yourself.'

'I *was* honest with you!' Her hands clasped together yet her chin tilted up provocatively. 'I never lied.'

Slowly he shook his head, pacing forward and finding raw satisfaction in the way she shifted, half stumbling back against the balustrade.

'You lied by omission, Rosalie. And you know it.' He scowled down into her face, challenging her to disagree. 'You must know we'd never have become lovers if I'd known who you were. Is that why you kept the truth from me?'

Her gaze slid from his and she half turned towards the sea. 'Of course not. I didn't plan to have an affair with you. That was *your* idea.'

'So why didn't you explain who you are? Why hide the truth unless you had an ulterior motive?'

He stepped closer, near enough to inhale her soft, enticing scent on the salty evening air. His nostrils flared and his chest rose as he breathed deep. Only yesterday he wouldn't have hesitated to reach out and pull her to him, nuzzle the pressure point at the base of her neck, taste her sweetness on his tongue as his hands divested her of those exquisite, unnecessary clothes.

Such a difference a day made!

Now he resisted her because she was forbidden to him. Yet his body thrummed with desire so potent, so keen that it was torture standing so damnably close to the paradise he knew he could find in her arms.

'I just wanted to be…me, I suppose. I didn't want the fuss that goes with being linked to royalty. It's important for me to be independent.' She shrugged and her hands spread before her as if pleading for understanding. 'Anyway, I don't see that it matters. It wasn't important.'

'*Not important!*' His voice was a barely muted roar as he recalled the shaft of searing pain that had speared through him, transfixing him as he'd walked into the audience chamber and recognised her. The shock of recognition and thwarted desire had paralysed him in mid-stride.

How could she claim her true identity wasn't important when it was all that kept him from scooping her up into his arms and ravishing her right here, right now, against the sun-warmed stones?

Had she no conception of the intensity of his hunger for her?

She couldn't be that naïve. Not after what they'd shared. She had to know how he burned for her even now.

At last her eyes rose to his. In the fast-gathering gloom they looked sombre.

'You didn't need to know all about me,' she countered, her voice tight and bitter. 'You wanted me in your bed, that's all. You don't need to know every intimate detail about someone for that. And that's all there was between us, Arik. Sex. A casual affair—no strings attached. That's all there could ever be.'

Seconds ticked by as he exhaled. There was a rushing roar in his ears as his blood pumped faster. His fingers bit into his arms through the layers of his clothing as he fought the impulse to snatch her close and shake her till she recanted.

He breathed in so deeply that his chest ached.

He frowned, stunned to register such outrage at her words. Surely she was right. Sex was all he'd had on his mind at first. But now…

Now it wasn't enough.

His frown tilted into a scowl at his confused thoughts. It should be simple. Hers was the sort of logic he'd used time and again himself over the years. And yet somehow, *now*, it was flawed.

'You have a very low opinion of me, of men, if you think there's no more to us than the need for a quick lay. Didn't our time together tell you anything about me? Don't you know there's more to me than my libido?' His voice was clipped, staccato with rage.

After all the patience, the tenderness he'd shown with her, he was sullied by her accusation.

If she'd been right then he'd have seduced her that first day, as he knew he could have, ignoring her protestations and her caution, using his body and her weakness for it, to get what he wanted. It would have been fast and furious and fantastic. But not as mind-numbing as the exquisite lovemaking they'd eventually shared.

He stalked to the balustrade and gripped the stonework so hard that it bit into his palms. He was furious with her for the implied insult. And with himself for the knowledge that she'd been all too correct in her reading of his original motives. He *had* wanted nothing more than her sensuous, delightful body against his.

He lashed out furiously, remembering the malicious gossip he'd heard at the reception. 'Or is it *you* who can't bear the thought of sharing with a man? Of trusting one? Is that it, Rosalie? Are you scared of what might happen if you open yourself?' He turned and fixed her with a glare. 'Is that what happened to Amy's father? Did you tell *him* it was only about physical need?'

Her raw gasp was loud in the throbbing silence. Her eyes were glazed with shock as she stared up at him. Instantly he regretted his words. It was his frustration speaking. He'd never felt such a flood of unrestrained wrath. She was a soft target for his anger, but he knew he should direct his fury at himself.

She slumped against the balcony rail as if her knees had given way and Arik stepped towards her, ready to catch her close as guilt seared him. But her outstretched hand barred him. That and the anguished twist of her mouth as she sucked in another laboured breath.

'No! Don't.' She shook her head so that her unbound hair swirled round her face.

He watched as she braced herself on the stonework, her gaze fixed on the sea. Even from this angle, in the fading light, he could read the bitterness in her tight mouth.

It was the hardest thing he'd done, holding back from her when she was in such a state. Even harder than resisting her sensual allure.

'Maybe you're right,' she said at last in a voice he didn't recognise. 'Maybe it's me that's the problem. Do you think so?' She turned her head to meet his gaze and the sight of her drawn face made his gut clench.

She turned away again, fixing her eyes on the distant horizon. When she finally spoke her voice was cool, uninflected, as if all emotion had faded away. 'But you're wrong about Amy's father. It wasn't like that.'

'I know, Rosalie. I—'

'You *can't* know. You have no idea.' She paused and drew a deep, shaky breath. 'So I'll tell you. Confession is supposed to be good for the soul, isn't it?'

Part of him wanted to reach out and fold his arms about her. To tell her there was no need to share a past that was so obviously painful to her. But he kept quiet. For his baser self wanted to hear it all. Even though he couldn't have what he wanted from her again. Even though she was taboo. Even though just standing here with her tested his self-control to the limits.

'A few years ago I left home and moved to Brisbane,' she said in a voice devoid of colour. 'I'd saved enough to go to art school there. I had no scholarship but I found a part time job and a tiny flat. I had dreams of becoming an artist.'

Her voice wobbled and searing heat pierced his chest at the sound of her pain.

'I suppose I was gullible in those days. Too trusting. I took people at face value and I was so thrilled to be learning about art that I didn't have much time for anything else.' She paused so long that he thought she wouldn't go on.

'I'd never even had a boyfriend. Not a real one. You could say I was a late bloomer when it came to interest in the opposite sex.' She laughed then, the sound mirthless and grating.

Arik's hands clenched white-knuckled on the stonework as he forced himself to listen and not gather her close. There was such distress in her voice.

'And then, in my second semester in Brisbane, there was a guy.' Her breath eased out in a long sigh. 'He was…different. Even the way he looked at me was different; it made me feel…special.'

Arik cursed himself for a fool, forcing her into these memories. He didn't want to hear about her past lovers. Yet he couldn't tear himself away.

'At first he didn't seem to notice me, not properly. And then one day he asked me out. He was going to a party that night and he wanted me to go too.' She was breathing faster now, her words coming quickly.

'It was at a big two-storey house. A mansion. I'd never been inside a place like it. There were so many rooms. And people everywhere. Lots of shouting and music. People having a good time.'

Arik moved closer, concerned at the way her breath came in rough pants. At the clipped unnatural rhythm of her voice.

'Rosalie? You don't have to—'

'I had a cocktail and we stood out on the balcony, a huge group of us, talking about art and galleries and our prospects for the future. It was great…' Her voice petered out and Arik saw her close her eyes.

'It was great to start with. But then I started to feel sick. Woozy. Someone suggested the drink had been a bit too strong and I needed to lie down.' She swallowed down hard.

'I don't even remember making it off the balcony. I just remember someone supporting me, holding me. And then, nothing.'

The silence was thick between them, taut with the weight of her memories and his sudden sense of foreboding.

She opened her eyes and clasped her hands on the railing before her.

'When I woke it was morning.' Her voice wobbled so much that she had to stop. Her shoulders heaved and then she angled her chin up, staring out at the darkening sea. 'When I woke I was naked. The bed was a tangled mess and I was…bruised. I'd been raped.'

Arik heard her words ring out defiantly and felt something whack into his abdomen. A sensation of swooping distress. Of helpless rage.

For long minutes silence throbbed between them.

'Did you press charges?' he asked when he eventually found his voice.

She shook her head. 'I had no idea who was responsible. Whether it was the guy who took me there or someone else. And I felt…soiled; all I wanted to do was get home. Get away. I couldn't face the prospect of an investigation. All those people being questioned. All of them finding out.'

'It wasn't your fault, Rosalie.' The words emerged through his gritted teeth. The fire in his belly, the adrenaline in his bloodstream needed an outlet. He wished he'd been there to deal with the scum responsible. His fury was blood-hot. Violent.

Instead he turned and, with infinite gentleness, drew her into his arms. He held his breath, waiting for her to protest, to shrink away. It felt so incredibly good when she didn't. At least she trusted him to comfort her.

'I know it wasn't my fault.' Her voice was muffled against his chest and her face buried in his shirt. The heat of her breath on his body eased just a fraction of the desolate emptiness he felt. 'But I wasn't strong then. Not like now. I was scared.'

His arms tightened around her, gathering her against him. He wished he could wipe the pain from her mind. Hell! He wished he'd never opened his mouth. He'd been so ready to fling thoughtless accusations.

'And then I found out I was pregnant.' There was more pain in her breaking voice than he'd ever heard. He tucked her close under his chin and rocked her against him.

'It's all right, Rosalie.'

'It is now,' she whispered. 'At first it wasn't. At first I didn't want the baby. I thought she'd just remind me of what had happened. But then, when she was born, it was different. I love her so much. She's a part of me and I'll never let anything come between us.'

She sniffed and drew back in his arms. Reluctantly he released her as she stepped away. Cool air replaced her warmth against his chest.

His arms felt empty without her.

'Amy's all I need in my life.' She lifted her face to look at him and he could make out the shimmer of tears glazing her eyes. The sight twisted pain through his chest, clamping down on his roughly pulsing heart.

'But when you offered me…passion, I couldn't resist. I was curious. I wanted to find out for myself what it was like. I wanted to know, to have what I'd never had before.'

In all his life Arik had never felt such a heel. In the face of her trauma, her need for solace, his own physical desire was a shallow thing, his scheme to get her into his bed shamefully selfish.

He stared down at her, seeking some sign of animation in her blank face. But there was nothing. No pain, no regret, no emotion at all. The sight of that nothingness brought piercing sorrow. He felt the rusty taste of raw emotion in his throat, the salt tang of distress that he hadn't tasted since childhood with the loss of his father. His chest felt tight and full as if his heart were about to burst out of his body.

'What we shared was wonderful,' Rosalie whispered in a voice devoid of all emotion. 'Thank you, Arik. But it's time for me to get back to my *real* life. To my responsibilities and my daughter.'

Her words had the ring of finality, like metal slamming down, echoing endlessly into emptiness.

She moved away from him, slipping silently out of his reach like a ghost.

The wooden door grated on its hinges as she left.

And then there was nothing but the shushing of the waves on the shore far below and the voice of his conscience castigating him for a thoughtless, selfish brute.

# CHAPTER ELEVEN

FOR the first time in years Rosalie slept late next morning, waking groggy and thick-headed to bright sunlight and the sound of birdsong.

Surprisingly, she hadn't tossed and turned, replaying memories in her mind, reliving old fears and pain. Nor had last night's confrontation with Arik kept her awake. It was as if both mind and body had finally shut down, allowing her a night's respite from the emotions that plagued her.

Instead, as she'd eased into slumber, she'd remembered the strong curve of Arik's arms around her. The solid masculine heat of his body against hers as he held her close. The steady thump of his heart beneath her cheek as she'd let herself lean into him. The comfort she'd drawn from his concern and his protective embrace.

That had been enough to dispel the old anxieties that had once stalked her nights.

She'd felt drained, exhausted and, finally, at peace.

But now, stretching in the bright morning sun, Rosalie realised that peace had been an illusion.

It was still there, nagging at her, refusing to be silenced: the truth she'd been avoiding for days.

*The fact that she'd fallen in love.*

Even now, just acknowledging it to herself, her heart gave a little fluttery thump.

She'd given in to temptation, had entered into an affair despite her better judgement, and look what had happened.

She was in love with Arik Ben Hassan.

A man she'd only met last week.

The man she knew intimately.

A man who was arrogant and proud and expected always to get his own way.

The man who'd been tender and gentle and who'd tempered his urgent need in the face of her fears and caution.

A man who had the sensual expertise of a true sybarite. A man whose past was littered with mistresses and filled with luxury.

The man who'd made her feel as if she were the centre of his world. As if no woman could compare with her.

A man with the wealth to enjoy life as a carefree playboy, in a world far removed from the harsh realities of her own life.

The man who worked hard, not because he needed to, but because it was his duty to support his people. And because he'd never be content to live aimlessly.

The man who made her *feel* so much.

She turned and buried her face in her pillow as the burning tide of despair welled in her.

She wanted the impossible. She wanted him to want her, to feel just a tiny spark of the love she felt for him.

She wanted the fairy tale.

But it was out of the question. She'd been a passing fancy. A woman to while away the hours till he returned to his fast-paced life. He'd told her a little about his world—the travel, the busy schedules. No doubt he'd been at a loose end for all those weeks, recuperating at home. She'd been an amusing interlude to alleviate the boredom.

Now he was angry that she'd left him high and dry. He

wasn't accustomed to women deserting him before he was ready to say goodbye.

She remembered the imposing angle of his high cheekbones, the plane of his jaw, the quirk of his mobile mouth, the sensual intensity of his sizzling regard, and knew he must spend his life fighting off would-be lovers. That was why he was annoyed—because he was used to calling the shots.

With his devastating charm, his sensational body and his wealth, Arik was a man who got his own way. Every time.

It was pique that had driven him to confront her last night. Pique and curiosity.

She swallowed down on the knot of bitter memory filling her throat.

Well, she'd satisfied his curiosity. She'd told him about her past. And she remembered only too well the look of horror on his shadowed face. It had wiped the anger and the remnants of lust from his expression.

Now he knew her for what she was: a woman permanently damaged by a past she couldn't change. A woman who battled every day to build a positive life for herself and her daughter. Who couldn't rely on romantic dreams.

Abruptly she sat up and pulled her hair from her face.

That was one thing she knew about: independence.

Her father had walked out on the family when she was just a kid, breaking her heart. His desertion had made her draw in upon herself, living in a sheltered fantasy world where everything turned out all right in the end. She'd been reserved, introspective, finding hope and reassurance in her art. Then even that had been stolen from her when she'd been abused and assaulted. She'd almost given up the struggle then, knew her mother had worried for her very survival. But then Amy had come along and with that her own salvation.

Rosalie had become a mother and from that point had worked with dogged determination to drag herself out of the quagmire of fear and misery that haunted her. The future was hers to build for herself. For her and Amy.

That was all she needed. Her independence. The love of her daughter, her family.

And now, miraculously, she had her art again too. The power that had been denied her in the darkest days of despair had been given back to her.

She didn't need a man to be whole.

Rosalie flung back the covers and glanced at the other bed in the room. It was empty. Amy had already left for the stables and her early morning visit to the puppies.

For a moment anxiety speared through Rosalie, then she realised Amy would never be alone, not here. She suspected the servants actually waited, on watch for the little tot to appear. Amy would have at least one of the stable hands and probably more, looking after her.

Nevertheless, Rosalie swung her legs out of bed quickly. She'd feel better when she was with Amy. And her daughter would keep her busy enough that, with luck, she wouldn't have time to think about Arik.

She'd never see him again. No way would he come back to the palace to see Rafiq while she was here. It would be too uncomfortable for him. No doubt he was already planning his next trip to the Far East or the new offshore oil rigs he'd mentioned.

How long would it take the pain of her lost hope to ease?

Giggles echoed through the dim building as Rosalie entered the vast stable. Instinctively she turned towards the direction of her daughter's laughter, only to pause at the sound of a deep voice, murmuring something she couldn't catch. It slipped like warm treacle across her skin, drawing a ripple of reaction from her.

Arik! She'd know his voice anywhere.

That shivery sensation in the pit of her stomach, the way

her nipples budded and tightened and her short uneven breathing: they were all dead giveaways.

What was he doing here? He should have returned home now, surely? Little Adham's birthday celebration was over and there was nothing more to keep him here, especially after what she'd told him last night.

But there was no mistaking the timbre of that voice.

She sagged back against the wall, her knees quivering and her pulse racing. She could no more persuade herself not to react to him than she could fly. Arik was like a lodestone, tugging at her senses, drawing her inevitably towards him.

All the more reason to get away as soon as she'd collected her daughter.

Rosalie straightened her shoulders and lifted her chin. Her hands were clammy and she tucked them into the pockets of her jeans. Then she stepped forward with what she hoped was an air of casual curiosity.

'If I lift you, you have to promise not to shout or wave your arms around,' said Arik in a voice that melted something vital inside her. 'Okay?'

''Kay.' Amy's voice was breathless with excitement and Rosalie automatically quickened her pace.

'There,' said Arik. 'Hold your hand out like this. Steady. Let her come to you. If you move suddenly you'll scare her and we don't want that, do we?'

'No. We don't want that,' Amy solemnly repeated.

Rosalie reached the stalls at the end of the building in time to hear Amy giggle shrilly and see her daughter held high in Arik's arms, totally absorbed in the sight of an enormous mare, leaning out from her stall towards her.

'She tickles!'

'Yes, I know, she's breathing on your hand,' Arik explained, 'sniffing to see if you have any food. Would you like to feed her?'

'Yes!'

'Yes, *please*, Amy.' It was her mother's voice correcting Amy from Arik's other side.

'Yes, *please*.'

But from here Rosalie saw only her daughter, focused totally on the horse, and Arik, the strong lines of his face softening as he looked down at Amy.

A twist of something almost like pain circled low in Rosalie's stomach, seeing the gentle approval on his hard, handsome face. Seeing her precious daughter held so protectively in his powerful arms. It pulled her up short just as she reached them.

'Then you may feed her since you ask so nicely. Here you are.' Arik passed Amy a piece of apple. 'No, not that way. Keep your hand flat and Saki will take it from you.'

He held Amy's hand steady in his own so the mare could snuffle up the treat. 'That's it. Perfect! Have you done this before?'

'No. Never!' Amy's voice was excited. 'Again! Please?'

'Of course you may. You fed her just right.'

'Can I ride her? Auntie Belle and Uncle Rafi ride.'

Instinctively Rosalie opened her mouth to intervene but it wasn't necessary. Arik was already answering.

'When you're old enough, perhaps you can ride.'

'When's that?'

'When your mother says so,' Arik responded. 'Here's some more apple you can give to Saki. Are you ready?'

'Mm hm!' Amy concentrated on balancing the apple on her palm, giggling when the mare daintily extracted it from her hand.

'Wait till your mother sees how well you do this,' said Arik. 'I know she'll be impressed.'

'I certainly *am* impressed.' Rosalie pasted a tense smile on her face and walked up to the group, careful to keep her attention on Amy, not the man who held her.

'Mummy, Mummy, did you see?' Amy swung round so fast that she startled the mare who jerked her head away. Instantly Arik turned his shoulder, putting himself between Amy and the animal.

'I saw, sweetheart. You've done very well. I think Saki must like you. Have you thanked Arik for letting you feed her?'

'Thank you,' Amy said with a wide grin as she looked up at him.

Rosalie saw a flash of expression on Arik's dark face, then he smiled back. 'You're welcome, little one.'

'Arik has been entertaining Amy for the best part of an hour.' It was Rosalie's mother speaking as she moved round to greet her. 'First with the puppies, then a visit to the peacock house and now a tour of the horses.'

Amy nodded vigorously and Rosalie watched her golden curls bob and swirl against the pale blue of Arik's shirt. If she moved her gaze a fraction she'd meet his eyes. But that was best avoided. She focused instead on the deeply tanned column of his throat.

'That's very kind of you—'

'It was entirely my pleasure. Amy is delightful.' He raised his hand to untangle a curl that had caught on his shirt button. Rosalie watched his long fingers deftly dislodging the long strands and swallowed hard.

Unbidden memories rushed back. Of him stroking the length of her own hair, down over her shoulders and breasts, of him lifting the strands to his face and inhaling, telling her she smelled like sunshine and roses. Of his hands spearing through her hair as he held her close, tilting her head as he kissed her: passionately, endlessly, addictively.

Rosalie bit down on her lip, trying to break the spell of evocative memory that blindsided her.

'It's time to come inside now, Amy, and have some breakfast.' She held out her arms.

'Arik too?' Amy asked as she tumbled forward into her arms. Startled, Rosalie lifted her eyes to his, wondering what he was thinking. But once again his dark gaze was impenetrable. She saw a flicker of warmth but no more. Just a long steady look that made her tremble at the realisation of how close he stood to her. Close enough to reach out and stroke her cheek. If he'd wanted to.

'Sorry, Amy,' Arik answered, 'I'm going out. I promised your uncle Rafiq I'd try out one of his horses this morning. I'm going for a ride. Perhaps another morning we could breakfast together.'

'You're staying here?' Rosalie couldn't help it that the words sounded brusque.

Arik inclined his head, one eyebrow tilting up towards his hairline. 'That's right. Rafiq invited me to stay some time ago. Initially I thought I wouldn't be able to remain as I had another…commitment.' Sudden fire blazed in his eyes as he looked down at her and Rosalie felt the heat scorch right through her.

'But my plans have altered. I'll be here for at least a week.'

For a long moment his gaze held hers and her throat dried at the banked heat she saw there. Then he swung away with a nod to her mother and a blinding smile for Amy. 'I'll see you ladies later.'

*A week. A week in the same house as Arik!* Rosalie braced herself against the intense turmoil of emotions that rocked her. Fear, pain, anger…and excitement? No. She couldn't be so stupidly self-destructive as to welcome the opportunity to see him again. Not when the sight of him tore at her heart with razor claws.

She was in a daze as she walked back to the palace with her mum and Amy. She listened to their chatter and nodded and smiled at the appropriate times, but all the while she was aware of a deep sinking feeling in the pit of her stomach.

Arik would be at the palace for a whole week. And the look on his face told her he didn't intend to avoid her. How could she survive so long without giving herself away? Without betraying the depth of her feelings for him? Without tumbling into his arms and begging for just one more embrace? One final caress before they parted?

'And such a pleasant man too,' she heard her mother say. 'I had no idea you'd met someone while you were out painting.' She paused as if awaiting a response.

Rosalie shrugged and lifted Amy higher on her hip. 'It didn't seem important at the time.'

*Liar.*

'I didn't think I'd see him again.'

'And now you have. What a nice surprise for you both.'

Rosalie shot her mum a sideways glance. There was far more to that observation than trite chat and those penetrating blue eyes were fixed on her intently. Her mother had always seen far too much, especially where she was concerned. The stress of the last few years meant that Maggie Winters kept a close protective eye on her younger daughter.

Rosalie knew her family had watched her and Arik with avid curiosity last night. No doubt they'd spent the evening speculating on the relationship between them for, despite her best efforts, she'd failed miserably in her attempts to appear as a polite stranger to him.

She'd seen the significant looks pass between her mum and Belle. Thank goodness they hadn't realised precisely how well *acquainted* she and Arik really were.

Rosalie shrugged. 'I don't suppose I'll see much of him. After his conversation with Rafiq last night, I gather he'll spend his time in the stables.'

But that was where she was wrong.

Over the days that followed it seemed Arik was everywhere she turned. He didn't overtly follow her but his presence was unavoidable. He was treated as one of the family, which meant sharing mealtimes. That was a torment she couldn't escape, not unless she wanted her eagle-eyed sister and her mum to worry that she was unwell.

Every morning when she took an insistent Amy to the stables to visit the animals, he was there, just in from a ride or chatting with Rafiq about horse-breeding. And every morning he'd stop what he was doing to spend time with Amy.

The sight of her little girl, so eagerly seeking his company, and he, so patently good with kids, made her feel dangerously soft and mushy inside. He'd make a great father one day. When he finally decided it was time to settle down with one of his glamorous society girlfriends or maybe a royal princess.

But it wasn't only in the early mornings that he invaded her peace. It seemed that, wherever she wandered when Amy was asleep, there he was: in the heavily scented tropical garden, chatting with her family, reading newspapers in the library or doing laps in the magnificent azure pool.

More than once she'd stopped there, hidden in the shadows, her heart in her mouth as she'd watched him power the length of the pool, then turn with a supple jackknife and plough back down the lane. The water rippled from his broad shoulders, his dark hair plastered to his skull and the curve of his rising arms made her itch for her crayons so she could capture the sheer energy of him on paper.

The sight of him enthralled her—and not just because he'd make a perfect model. Her interest in his magnificent physique was much more *personal* than that.

She spent more and more time in her room or playing alone with Amy, till her mum started to question whether she was all right and she was forced to make an appearance and join the family party.

Which inevitably meant being with Arik, for he was one

of the family. He and Rafiq had grown up together, had shared a lifetime's experiences. Even her sister, Belle, had a soft spot for him. He'd been one of Belle's first friends in Q'aroum and the sight of her and Arik, laughing together, was enough to turn Rosalie's mood sour.

Rosalie's feelings when she saw the two of them together confounded her. She couldn't be jealous of Belle. She knew her sister was head over heels in love with her own handsome husband. But that didn't stop the green-eyed demon of jealousy popping up when Rosalie saw how close Belle and Arik were, how comfortable together. There was an ease between them that she would never share with him.

How much she longed to be able to relax in Arik's company. Enjoy his wit and his conversation without feeling guilty because she wanted what she shouldn't, couldn't have. No matter how many times she told herself to be strong, it was impossible to stifle her hopeless yearning.

Worse still, her family patently approved of him. Who wouldn't? He was courteous, amiable, attentive, a great conversationalist, but a man who listened as well.

Rosalie sighed. He was so darned near perfect! Even his single-minded determination to get what he set his mind to was a plus. Belle called it strength of character and described how much he'd done to stimulate investment and research in alternative energies, the multitude of community support programmes he'd initiated and his energetic plans for local reform.

Rosalie wondered what her sister would say if she knew he'd turned that formidable focus on to the task of seducing her kid sister. Even now she shivered at the forbidden memory of his hot, hungry gaze and his possessive touch.

If Rosalie had to listen to her family sing his praises much longer she thought she'd explode!

It wasn't that she disagreed with them. He *was* a most remarkable man. That was precisely the problem. She didn't want to be reminded again and again of what she couldn't have. Each day, each hour was torture, not knowing when or how they'd be flung together again. Time and again at meals she found herself trapped next to him at the table, over-whelmed by the sensations his proximity aroused.

*Aroused.*

Now there was a word that said it all. No matter how often she told herself the affair was over, she couldn't dispel the secret shivery excitement of her betraying body. She only had to hear his dark velvet voice, scent his skin as he leaned close to pass her something or feel his eyes on her across a room and her body jangled with excitement. Ready. Waiting. Wanting.

It infuriated her almost as much as it scared her. Would she ever get over her feelings for him? Finally, devastatingly she'd fallen in love. And now she wondered if there was any way out. Surely she wasn't doomed to suffer this maelstrom of longing and despair for the rest of her life?

If only she could escape. Get away from the stress of pretending to enjoy herself when all the while she yearned desperately for the man who was so patently beyond her reach. The keenness of her pain caught her breath, especially when she turned suddenly to see him watching her, his face brooding and his eyes shuttered.

What went on behind that mask of control? Was he still angry with her? Or did he remember only her ugly story of violence and lost innocence? Did he pity her for what she'd suffered? The idea snagged at her wounded ego.

Either way it didn't matter. Her future was set. Soon she'd return home and take up the threads of her real life. She wouldn't allow herself to yearn for the impossible.

# CHAPTER TWELVE

ROSALIE slipped through the door of her suite and into the wide passage. Amy had settled down for the night with one of the maids to watch over her and Rosalie didn't want her to wake. It had taken ages to get her daughter to sleep, partly because she was so excited, seeing her mum dressed up in unaccustomed finery.

Rosalie smoothed the satiny fabric of her new dress down over her hips, feeling the sensuous slide of it against her skin. It was a beautiful gift from Belle, with its delicately embroidered neckline, close-fitting bodice and the ultra-feminine swirl of long skirt. Just the sort of dress Rosalie would never have chosen for herself, but perfect for tonight's formal party.

That was one thing Rosalie would never envy her sister. She might have a gorgeous, loving husband, an adorable baby, the career she always wanted and a blessed life in a fairy tale palace, but the downside was the weight of public duty. This was the second formal reception at the palace in a week. Thank goodness Rosalie had no official role and could blend into the background.

She started down the corridor, hurrying a little despite the unfamiliar high heels, knowing she was late. At the first corner she turned left and straight into the arms of the man coming towards her.

This passageway was in unfamiliar darkness, but she knew immediately it was Arik. The grip of his hands on her arms, the subtle teasing scent of his skin, the familiarity of his body—all were unmistakable. As was her instant reaction. Her lungs emptied of air in a sudden rush and a tickle of awareness spread across her skin. Deep within her that insidious coil of desire twisted into life.

'You can let me go.' Was that her voice, breathless and uneven? She stepped back and his hands fell away.

In the gloom she couldn't make out his expression but she felt his gaze on her face. She lifted her chin.

'What's happened to the lights?'

'That's why I came to get you. Rafiq and Belle are already entertaining the first guests.' In contrast to her voice, his was calm and even. 'You remember the workmen rewiring this older section of the building today? Well, it seems they haven't quite fool-proofed the new circuits. The next few corridors are blacked out and it may take a while to locate the problem.'

Of course. There could be no personal reason for him to search her out. Yet her pulse hammered in her throat when she stood so close to him.

It was the first time they'd been alone together since the evening she'd revealed the secrets of her past.

Is that what he was thinking about as he stood unmoving, his head inclined towards hers? Tension stiffened her shoulders, gripped her chest in a vice that snatched her breath.

Not his pity. Not that!

She sidestepped his looming bulk and paced forward into the darkness. Now her eyes had adjusted she saw silvery light ahead, moonlight spilling in through the high windows.

He fell into step beside her and she felt the warmth of his body press close. His hand reached for hers and folded it in the crook of his elbow. She faltered and would have stumbled but for his support.

'Stay by me, Rosalie. That way there'll be no mishaps.'

'But I can see my way well enough!' She tugged to be free, a useless effort since he kept her clamped close to his side. She felt the fine cotton of his shirt beneath her fingers, the fleeting caress of his long cloak against her bare ankle. And his heat. How could she have forgotten the intensity of the warmth that spread from his muscled body, teasing her even through their clothes?

'You're safer with me.'

'I'm perfectly capable of walking unsupported!'

His pace slowed and, perforce, hers did too. 'You find my presence so objectionable?' His words were crisp, deliberate, yet she couldn't decipher that particular inflection. Was it anger?

'Is that why you continually avoid me?' Now he stopped and turned towards her, his shoulders blocking the bright slabs of moonlight from view.

'I don't avoid you. I—'

'Don't lie, Rosalie. You're very bad at it.'

She sucked in a stunned breath and stared up into the darkness that was his face. What did this man *want* from her? Surely he was grateful she hadn't played the clinging vine? That she hadn't embarrassed them both in front of her family and his cousin.

Just as well he didn't have a clue how much the façade of disinterest cost her. Even now pain was welling inside.

'Let me go, please. I prefer to walk alone.' She couldn't help the tremor in her tone, but at least she sounded calm.

For answer he swung round and pulled her forwards, pacing fast down the corridor. 'And I prefer that we take this opportunity to talk. *Alone.* Whenever I come near you, you scurry away. You continually find excuses to put distance between us.'

Rosalie's jaw dropped. 'There's nothing to talk about. It's over between us,' she hissed, stumbling a little as his pace lengthened and he tugged her towards the dark side of the corridor.

'Nothing to discuss?' His voice grated, a harsh whisper just above her ear. Then he lunged to one side, thrust open a door and tugged her into a darkened room.

'What are you doing?' Nerves made her voice thin.

'Making sure we're alone.'

Emphatically she shook her head. 'No! Belle and Rafiq are expecting us. We need to go now.' There was nothing left to say to Arik. Nothing she *trusted* herself to say.

'No one will miss us. And it's past time we sorted this out.'

Rosalie stepped back into the gloom, straight into the back of a padded sofa. 'There's nothing to sort out. We had an affair. It's over. Now we go our separate ways.'

He paced closer, a threatening bulk looming blacker than the shadows of the moonlit room. She bit her lip and stood straighter, her fingers digging into the upholstery behind her.

'You cannot be so naïve as to believe that, Rosalie.' His voice had the seductive quality of rich, dark chocolate, his accent suddenly more pronounced, its lilt making her stomach dip in unwanted excitement.

'It's the truth!'

*The truth.*

What *was* the truth about him and this woman?

She was like wildfire in his blood. He wanted her in his bed; in fact, he craved her anywhere he could get her, with such a driven need that he was in perpetual torment. He couldn't put her out of his mind, no matter how sternly he reminded himself of the barriers between them. Yet, despite the consuming rush of lust, his need was greater even than that. He wanted to hold her, comfort her, protect her. Her pain was his, he *felt* her hurts in his blood, his bones, his very marrow. It was as if he'd absorbed her anguish into himself. No wonder he felt ripped asunder every time he remembered the fresh pain he'd caused her with his thoughtless words the other night.

What did it mean?

This was beyond even his experience. And if there was one thing he could claim, it was experience of women.

All he knew was that he couldn't drag himself away as he was duty-bound to do. He was like some damned satellite, orbiting, coming tantalisingly close to a bright, beckoning star and then veering off into darkness again.

It couldn't go on. This situation had to be resolved.

'We need to talk, Rosalie.' Somehow he'd sort this out, break the unseen ties that bound them so he could do what he must and walk away from her.

She shook her head and her long unbound hair swirled around her head. In the gloom it rippled like silver, but he knew it to be the colour of gold, warm and silkily seductive to the touch.

His hands clenched as he resisted the impulse to reach out and slide his hand down those tresses, over her shoulder and her breast. Too dangerous. He needed to keep a cool head.

But already she was moving away, heading for the door.

He spun round as she reached for the handle.

'No!'

She ignored him, tugging the door towards her.

His splayed hand slammed down on the heavy wood just above her shoulder, thrusting it shut.

'Arik. Open the door, please. I want to leave.'

He heard the waver in her low voice and almost relented. The tension came off her in waves and he had to repress the urge to comfort her as he wanted to, with her tucked in against his chest and his arms holding her tight. This close he could smell the fresh scent of her skin, the sunshine smell of her soap, sparking intimate memories.

He couldn't afford to be sidetracked.

'We need to talk, Rosalie. That's all.'

There was a flurry of movement as she spun round to face

him. Her pale face looked up into his. He heard her breaths, short and sharp, and his pulse quickened. With his arm still holding the door shut, they stood far too close for clear thinking. But he couldn't move away. Not yet.

'Don't you listen?' The words were harsh, rising on emotion. 'There's nothing for us to discuss. It's over. Done. Finished. There's nothing between us any more, Arik.'

Some tiny voice in his mind told him she was lashing out to protect herself. But the sound of it was drowned by the urgent clamour of blood pounding in his head. By the surge of molten fury that suddenly gripped him.

*Finished!* She had to be kidding.

He'd tried all damned week to end this torment. To do what had to be done—to turn his back on her. And yet something held him back.

Never before had he found it impossible to do his duty.

He raised his other hand to her cheek, let the back of his fingers brush feather-light over her warm flesh.

Her sigh, stifled as she snapped her mouth shut, echoed the deep, slow, satisfied release of air from his own lungs. He'd wanted to reach out to her all week. Now, as his hand turned and he palmed the soft skin of her cheek, he wondered how he'd resisted for so long.

'It's not over, Rosalie. Not while there's *this* between us.'

'It has to be!'

Her hair caressed his hand as she shook her head. Her fingers were warm, supple and inviting as they closed on his hand, slid down to his wrist. But then suddenly she was tugging, trying to pull his hand away. Her grip grew more urgent and he allowed her to raise his hand a few centimetres from her face.

'This is your ego talking, Arik. You just don't want to admit it's over because *I* was the one who left *you*.'

Her words struck him with the force of a blow. For he knew

instantly that once that might have been the case. Once he might have felt his masculine pride had been dented by her ending their affair.

But this was something else. This was something—more.

His breathing snagged as the force of what he felt rocked him. It blasted through him like an explosion of red-hot lava. Good intentions, common sense, his careful plans, all obliterated in a scorching blaze of raw emotion.

'So there's nothing between us.' He didn't recognise the hoarse voice as his own. But nor were these aggressive, blatantly possessive instincts familiar as he looked down into her pale face.

He gathered her wrists in his hand and yanked them high over her head, hearing her hiss of surprise as if from a distance. He let his other hand trail over her face, his thumb pressing against her lips, parting them as his fingers cupped her cheek.

The air sizzled with static electricity. If there were a naked flame here Arik thought he'd ignite. Just the touch of her flesh against his, the warmth of her breath on his hand, had him burning up.

He opened his mouth to accuse her of lying, when her tongue, warm and wet and flagrantly seductive, grazed his thumb.

He groaned as the fire in his belly shot straight to his groin. That single caress brought him to instant, rampant readiness. His whole body stiffened and shook as she sucked his thumb into her mouth. Darts of fire speared into his belly, his chest, his legs. Instinctively he widened his stance, locking his knees against the ripples of desire shuddering through him.

In the shadows his eyes met hers. They were huge, staring up at him unblinking, inviting. Capitulating.

He didn't remember releasing his hold on her wrists but he must have for her breast was soft and pouting beneath his touch. Her fingers cupped his other hand at her mouth, slid up his wrist, then further, along his arm and back again. Her movements were restless, edgy, feeding the raw desire that surged within him.

Arik let his hand slide from her mouth, over her chin, her delicate bare neck, past the frantically racing pulse to her collar-bone, her other breast.

His mouth twisted in a tight smile as she pushed forward into his hands, filling them with her luscious feminine bounty.

'You still need me.' His voice grated out of his dry throat. 'Don't you, Rosalie?'

Her eyes closed as he squeezed her breasts and he watched her head loll back against the door, her neck curving in an erotic, inviting arch.

He lowered his head, allowing himself to be engulfed in the hot, heady scent of her, and licked the warm skin at her collar-bone.

She shuddered and he slipped his hands round her, tugging her close.

'Yes.' It was a sigh of a word, barely audible.

'Say it, Rosalie,' he demanded as he nuzzled the gossamer-thin silk of her bodice. He needed to hear her admit it. His lips closed over one thrusting nipple and he sucked hard. She bucked in his arms, her hands braced on his shoulders, her fingers digging into him. Deliberately he drew her close, flush against the iron hardness of his lower body.

'I need you, Arik.' It emerged as a desperate sob that incited immediate action. His hands moved automatically, scrabbling at her long skirts, thrusting them up so he could anchor himself against her.

Of course it wasn't enough. His chest heaved, his breathing coming too fast as he fumbled at his trousers.

Her hands were on him now, distracting him as they attacked his shirt, wrenching buttons undone till he felt the warmth of her palms against his skin.

Yes!

Finally he was free of the restricting clothes. He reached out to her, found the delicate wisp of fabric barring his entry to paradise and tore it away in a single ripping tug.

Hot, soft flesh, the graze of silky hair, moist heat. His breath stopped in his lungs as he explored her intimately, felt her body jerk against his hand, heard her breath stop on a gasp of excitement.

No time now for words. For finesse. Arik knew only the instinct for fulfilment. To take this woman and claim her as his own. Incontrovertibly. Undeniably. Completely. In the surest way a man could claim a woman.

'Please, Arik.' Her arms were wrapped around him, drawing him to her.

He closed his hands on the curve of her waist, dimly aware of a primitive satisfaction at the way the neat indentation fitted his grasp. He lifted her up, pushing her back against the door and positioned himself right…there.

Her legs wrapped round him, tugging him closer. And now Rosalie anchored her hands at the back of his neck. Her fingers splayed through his hair.

It took just one decisive thrust, long and sure and perfect, to take him home.

The world stood still as he dragged in a breath, dimly aware that he ought to slow down. He should—

'Yes!' Her voice was the merest echo of sound in his ear, yet it shattered the last of his faltering control. Every muscle tensed, flexed as he bucked against her, surging high and deep and hard.

Arik's lips moved against the delicate curve of her ear as he described to her in an unbroken stream of words how good she felt. He told her exactly what he intended to do with her as he thrust into her again and again.

The flow of Arabic became slower, less fluent, broken, as

their bodies moved together, found a frantic, urgent rhythm that took control of them, gripped them and pounded them together against the door.

Rosalie welcomed him, pulled him tighter, further, till the world spun and colours flared and their rhythm raced out of control. Ecstasy. A barrage of exquisite sensation. It could have been the end of the world and Arik wouldn't have cared. For here, now, in his arms, he held all that he needed.

He pulsed hard inside her, the very essence of him flooding deep within her, filling her. And he knew that, beyond everything, this was *right*.

He held her, slumped and panting, against his chest as the last tremors died away. It hurt to breathe, the oxygen scoured his lungs, but he didn't care. He never wanted to let her go.

But all too soon her splayed hands were pushing at his chest. Her legs unlocked their intimate hold and she was wriggling, trying to slide down to the floor. Her long hair hid her down bent head, but he could hear her uneven breathing, feel her body's shivers in the aftermath of ecstasy.

He smiled, stepping back and lowering her. Even now the sensation of her delectable body easing down past his sated one brought the promise of future pleasure.

When she stood on her own feet he held her close for a moment before releasing her. Better to keep his hands to himself while they talked. Even after that cataclysmic orgasm, he didn't trust his libido around this woman. Her ability to arouse him, and to satisfy him, was unprecedented.

He was adjusting his clothes, trying to make himself look respectable again, when a sound froze his blood. Two sounds. The huge door creaking open almost drowned out the other noise, but not quite. Rosalie's anguished sob was enough to still his rapidly beating heart. His chest constricted painfully at the sound of her despair.

'Rosalie—' He reached for her but she was already hurtling away down the corridor. He stumbled over something—a pair of discarded shoes—and lost the opportunity to grab her.

Even so he would have pursued her if he hadn't heard the sound of her crying: raw and heartfelt. That stopped him in his tracks as surely as a spear through the chest.

*He'd* done that to her. With his demands, his violent passion, his insistence on getting his own way.

He *knew* how much Rosalie had been through. The rape, the fear and despair. How much she'd suffered. He'd sworn he'd keep his distance, just reason with her.

Yet there'd been no reason in his actions. He hadn't shown a shred of gentleness just now. He hadn't made love to the girl. He hadn't persuaded or seduced.

He'd demanded and ravaged.

Searing heat suffused his face as he recalled the desperate battering beat of his body slamming into hers, his hands tight and uncompromising on her delicate flesh as he'd slaked his lust with raw passion. No finesse. No tenderness.

It had been the most perfect sexual union of his life: And he'd been so sure it had been the same for her. But had he really bothered to find out?

All she'd wanted from the moment she'd cannoned into him was to get away. Surely she deserved to be left alone now.

Mechanically he buttoned his shirt, fastened his trousers, put her shoes neatly to one side. But as he bent he saw something pale on the floor. A scrap of white.

His fingers touched lace and automatically closed on the fabric. He couldn't leave Rosalie's underwear there, torn and tell-tale, to be discovered by one of the maids. Instead he shoved the scrap into his pocket, knowing a self-loathing so deep it stifled his breath.

How could he atone for what he'd done?

Could he ever make this right?

* * *

Fifteen minutes later, when he finally returned to the large reception room, Arik was conscious only of branding guilt. It was like a physical mark on his flesh, reminding him of his hubris. No plan had emerged from the seething mass of emotions and guilt. He felt punch-drunk on the enormity of what had just happened, and the unforgivable damage he'd inflicted on Rosalie.

He was barely aware of the colourful crowd closing in round him as he strode across the marble floor, intent on finding Rafiq and giving his excuses. He needed to be alone to sort this out.

His stride broke as he had to stop and skirt a middle-aged couple stepping across his path. His gaze flickered towards them as he heard a voice he recognised. Immediately he wished he hadn't. The man was a stranger to him but the woman he knew. She'd been the one spreading poison about Rosalie, just a week ago in this same room.

Automatically Arik halted, a sixth sense warning him of the need to beware.

Blood still pounded in his ears. That and the cacophony of voices had deafened him to any single conversation. Until now. Whispered words trickled into his ears, snatches half-masked by the crowd's hubbub.

*Déjà vu.*

'Bold as brass she was…but no husband, not that one…what damage she'll do to the reputation of the royal house…'

This time Arik was almost prepared for the salacious character assassination. And yet the woman's audacity was stunning. To speak so of Rosalie, here in the palace.

Last time he'd acted purely on gut instinct when he'd confronted the malicious gossip, hadn't even thought before the words were out of his mouth.

This time he stopped, absorbing the full impact of the ugly innuendo like a sickening body blow.

Out of the mind-numbing mass of half-formed thoughts

and guilty speculation that had plagued him since Rosalie had run away, certainty emerged. Absolute, bone-deep certainty. It came upon him in an instant of blinding insight, sudden and satisfying. He almost smiled his relief.

Instead he stuck his hands on his hips, planted his feet wide and looked down his nose at the plump pair wandering into his path. It was the fat husband who noticed him first, looking up, his jaw sagging his horror. Then the wife, her face paling and her words petering out as she took in the look on Arik's face.

Over their heads Arik caught an impression of decisive movement and looked up to see Rafiq striding purposefully through the crowd.

*Too late, cousin. I'll handle this once and for all.*

Arik stared down at the pair before him. He didn't bother to lower his voice. He had a point to make and the more that heard the better.

'I'd advise you to keep a still tongue in your head, woman.' She flinched at his tone, but he barely noticed. 'No one talks like that about the woman I plan to marry.'

# CHAPTER THIRTEEN

'YOU haven't asked me my intentions.' Arik met his cousin's eyes, knowing how much it cost Rafiq to keep his own counsel on this matter. After all, Rosalie was by marriage one of his womenfolk. It was Rafiq's duty to protect and care for her, especially when confronted with the man who'd seduced her and risked her public reputation.

Rafiq's expression was sombre in the early morning light. 'As if I don't know you as well as I know myself.' He paused, his look assessing. 'And it seems a night of contemplation hasn't changed your mind.'

Arik shook his head. A few sleepless hours hadn't altered the fundamental problem.

His cousin smiled then, a taut, quick curve of the lips. 'You know she's as stubborn as her sister? Totally independent?'

'I know.' Neither voiced the other issue: the fact that Rosalie Winters would hate Arik for what he'd done to her. He'd put her in an untenable position. The knowledge was like acid, eating away at Arik's conscience.

'I can give you probably fifteen minutes. But longer than that I can't promise. Belle won't want to let her out of her sight.'

Arik nodded. The window of opportunity was pitifully small. But it would have to do.

Both men turned at the sound of voices approaching across

the manicured lawn. A group emerged from the palace: Belle carrying little Adham, Amy skipping ahead, Mrs Winters and, in the centre, as if shielded by her relatives, Rosalie, looking pale and tired.

Something squeezed hard in Arik's chest as he took in the bruised shadows beneath her eyes and the droop of her shoulders. Guilt flagellated him, tearing at his flesh and seizing his breath.

'Uncle Rafi! Arik!' It was Amy who spotted them first, swerving away from the women and racing towards them across the grass.

Arik felt a hand on his shoulder and then Rafiq strode away towards his family. For the first time in his life Arik felt a pang of pure envy, watching Rafiq's pace quicken as he neared his wife and baby son. He saw Belle pause, reach out a protective arm towards her younger sister. But then Maggie Winters, her mother, was somehow between her daughters and urging Belle away, towards Rafiq.

Arik frowned. What did that gesture mean?

Then his mind clouded as he stared into Rosalie's huge, pained eyes. Even from here he could guess that they were grey rather than green. The colour of storms and anguish.

His breath rattled in his chest.

*He'd* done that to her.

Rosalie stumbled to a halt at the sight of Arik, tall and lean and utterly gorgeous, bathed in the golden glow of morning. He stood at the entrance to the stables, watching her. Her blood quickened. Despite everything, despite a night of silent admonition, she couldn't prevent her tell-tale reaction. The sheer excitement the sight of him generated in her betraying body.

It didn't matter that he only wanted her for sex. Had only ever felt lust for her: raw and primitive and barbarically glorious.

Her body didn't care. Just look at the way she'd responded to him last night. She'd been hungry for him, wanton and more than willing in her craving for him. Just the caress of his hand on her face, the scent and sound and feel of him standing so close to her in the dark had stripped away every defence, every last shred of control. She'd *invited* him to take her. She'd revelled in their urgent, almost violent coupling, up against a door of all places!

It had only been afterwards, when it had been too late, that she'd realised what she'd done. She'd thrown away her self-respect for steaming sex in the dark.

Heat scorched her cheeks as she dropped her gaze. But she couldn't hide from the truth. Despite everything, it was excitement that skittered through her body.

She bit her trembling lower lip. When would she learn to control these primitive emotions? The stupid, pointless yearning for a man who didn't need her?

Jerkily she lifted her chin, refusing to be cowed, only to see Amy veer past Rafiq and, straight as an arrow, catapult into Arik's arms.

Something hard and sharp jolted deep inside her at the sight of her precious little girl swung high in the arms of the man Rosalie needed to avoid at all costs. The man who could seduce her without trying, who held her heart in his hands and didn't even know it.

Seeing the pair together was a heartbreaking travesty of her hopeless, self-indulgent dreams—of Arik returning her love, wanting her, even accepting her daughter as his own.

'You'd better go with Amy to check on the pups,' said her mum's voice near her ear. 'You know she won't settle till she's seen them. We'll go on ahead to this picnic breakfast Rafiq has organised.'

Rosalie looked over to the picturesque pavilion where Rafiq's servants had carried platter upon platter of food.

Already Rafiq and Belle were walking ahead, deep in conversation, Rafiq with his arm wrapped lovingly around his wife.

Rosalie stifled a sigh. She had to face Arik some time. Better to do it with Amy there to keep things in perspective. Maybe this time she could persuade herself that she didn't care. That it had been no more than a meaningless holiday romance.

One day, surely, she'd come to believe it.

Her gait was stiff, her shoulders cramped with tension as she approached the stables. She could feel his eyes on her, hot as a brand, but she managed not to flinch.

'Are you ready to see the puppies, sweetheart?' Perhaps if she looked only at her daughter and avoided Arik's gaze, she could get through this.

'Uh huh.' Amy nodded vigorously and wriggled to be put down. But then, to Rosalie's horror, she reached up a hand to Arik and another to her.

Beside her she sensed Arik stiffen, clearly appalled at the unconscious intimacy of Amy's gesture. But then, a second later, Rosalie saw his strong, long-fingered hand engulf Amy's. Rosalie reached for her little girl's other hand, telling herself not to think about the picture they made. The strong, handsome man, the gorgeous little girl and the woman who loved them both. Almost like a family.

Rosalie swallowed down on the bitter taste of self-indulgent tears. She needed to stop this now! She was too strong for this. She'd never have survived the last few years if she'd allowed herself to languish in self-pity.

So she stifled the sob that rose in her throat and plastered an overbright smile on her face.

'Just a quick visit this time, Amy. Everyone's waiting to have breakfast with us.'

'Yes, Mummy.' But already Amy's attention was absorbed elsewhere as she knelt in the straw of the first stall, surrounded by a wriggling, furry mass of chubby pups.

Which left Rosalie standing alone with—

'Rosalie.' His voice was low, devastating in its ability to awaken needs she tried so firmly to repress. 'I need to tell you—'

'There's nothing to say,' she hissed, automatically edging aside.

'You're wrong, *habibti*—'

'Don't call me that!' Rosalie swallowed down a lump of pure emotion. No matter how easily the endearments came to him, she couldn't bear to have him call her sweetheart. Not when she knew it meant nothing to him.

For answer he reached out and grasped her hand in his. She tugged, desperate for some space between them, but she couldn't match his superior strength. Not without an undignified tussle that would draw Amy's attention and her curiosity.

His hand was warm and hard, engulfing hers in a hold that restrained and yet seemed almost caressing.

She had to get a grip and stop imagining things!

'So what is it you need to tell me?' She darted a savage look up at his shuttered face and then away. Even in her sudden anger she didn't trust herself to look at him.

'Last night—'

'I'd rather not talk about that.'

'Last night,' he continued, his voice terse and curiously devoid of expression, 'when I reached the reception, I discovered someone gossiping.' He paused and she heard him breathe deeply. 'About you.'

She jerked round to face him. What on earth was going on?

'About me?' She shook her head. Of all the things he could have said, this was the least expected. What sort of gossip could there be about her?

His eyes, hooded and darkly gleaming, held hers. 'About the fact that Amy has no father.'

Rosalie felt something plummet through her chest. Emotion. Indignation. Anger. Disbelief.

It was unbelievable!

'That's no one's business but my own,' she said through her clenched jaw, unable to credit the sort of maliciousness that would make an issue of that. Then she realised she wasn't at home any more. She was in a foreign country. A country where the customs and expectations were different to her own.

Nevertheless, *she* had nothing to be ashamed of!

'I have to tell you that I made it my business.'

'How?' Rosalie stilled as the hairs on her nape prickled. Only now did she begin to notice the tension humming through his big body and the rigid set of his broad shoulders. Something was very wrong.

There was silence for a long moment and Rosalie heard the thrum of her heartbeat, loud and heavy.

'I announced that you were under my protection. That we were going to wed.'

There was a sudden whooshing sound that had to be the air rushing from her lungs. His hand tightened on hers as her knees threatened to buckle and she swayed.

In front of them, totally oblivious to the bombshell Arik had just dropped, Amy giggled as one of the puppies stood up on its hind legs and licked her chin.

Rosalie stared, trying to bring her whirling thoughts into order. It was impossible. Unbelievable.

'You had no right.' She swung round and looked up into his stern, impenetrable face. He looked forbidding, his expression harsh, his nose arrogantly hewn, his jaw solid and uncompromising. Like a man carved of stone or shaped of unyielding metal. His eyes glittered bright as obsidian and just as hard.

'It was my duty to protect you.'

'Your *duty*!' Her voice rose on a screech of disbelief that made Amy look up for an instant.

'You *have* no *duty* towards me,' Rosalie whispered when she was in control of her voice again. What did he think she was? Some helpless weakling in need of a protector? 'I can fight my own battles.'

'And if I want to fight them with you?'

She shook her head, tugging to pull her hand from his grasp. For answer he reached for her other hand, holding her steady so she couldn't escape without drawing Amy's attention.

'Don't be absurd! I'm nothing to you.'

'You keep saying that.' His mouth twisted up in a smile that looked as if it hurt. 'And yet you're the woman I plan to marry.'

If he hadn't been holding her, Rosalie knew she would have slumped to the floor as her knees liquefied in shock. She stared up into his brooding face, but there wasn't a flicker of emotion to be seen there. Not even a flash of humour.

'That's not funny.' There was a quiver in her voice and she gulped, trying to get control of her voice-box.

'No, Rosalie. It's not funny.'

'You can't be so…antiquated as to expect me to marry you just to stop some stupid gossip.'

He tilted his head as if considering her words.

'You don't care what people say about you? About Amy?'

'Of course I care. But I'm not going to let some malicious tattle force me into anything so absurd as marriage.'

'So you see the idea of marriage to me as absurd?' His deep voice resonated with an inflection she couldn't identify. Something that twisted her insides into a knot of hard distress.

'I…' She floundered for a suitable lie.

'As wife of the Sheikh you would be beyond such recriminations. You would be respected. Revered even.'

She couldn't believe her ears. He was talking as if it were even remotely feasible. Her and him. Man and wife. She choked down on welling emotion, blinked back the haze of useless tears that threatened. Even in this ridiculous situation she couldn't divorce herself from her secret, utterly absurd yearning—for his love.

'It's academic,' she murmured brokenly, looking down at his strong hands holding hers. 'It's not going to happen.'

'Rosalie.' His fierce whisper made her head snap up. 'I *want* to marry you.'

She shook her head. This had gone beyond a joke. She knew him to be supremely self confident, sure of getting his own way. But he was an honourable man too. He could be tender and patient. He shouldn't treat her like this.

'Don't lie to me, Arik. It doesn't matter. Truly. I'll survive a bit of gossip.'

If he'd looked severe before, the stark, aristocratic cast of his features made him look utterly unapproachable now. His fingers tightened their grip till the blood pulsed heavily in her hands.

'You couldn't be happy living with me? Living here in Q'aroum?'

Rosalie squeezed shut her eyes. It was too much, being offered such temptation. Of course she could be happy here. She'd be in seventh heaven if Arik loved her as she did him. But that wasn't within the realm of possibility. Not even to someone who'd spent her early years perfecting the art of fantasising.

She'd learned her lesson well since then. She lived in the real world. She faced the truth, no matter how harsh. Rosalie snapped her eyes open.

'There's no question of us marrying. It would have been better if you'd said nothing last night.' For surely he'd put himself in an invidious position, announcing a marriage that wasn't going to happen. It was *his* reputation he should worry about, not hers.

'You will not marry me?'

It was too much. Even for a woman who'd resolved not to show how much it hurt. Rosalie tasted blood on her tongue. She ducked her head, unable to meet his shuttered gaze any longer.

'Don't! Please, just…don't.'

'Rosalie? *Habibti.*' His arms came round her, tugging her resisting form close till she stood in his arms, felt the generous heat of his body encircling her.

Numbly she shook her head. The whole idea was crazy.

'I'm going home to Australia soon, anyway.' No matter what outmoded ideas prevailed in Q'aroum, they didn't apply in Australia.

'Then I shall follow you.'

What? Stunned, she looked up into his face. Never before had he looked so grim.

'I don't understand. Why would you—?'

'If that's where you are, then that's where I'll be. You should know by now that I'm a man who doesn't give up when he wants something.' He looked down at her and this time she saw a flicker of strong emotion on his features.

'I want you, Rosalie. And I intend to have you.'

'No!' What sort of game was this? 'It's over, Arik. I don't want an affair. I can't go on like this any more.'

'Nor can I, little one. This is tearing me apart.' His hand cupped her cheek, his thumb brushing across her lips in a caress that made her quiver deep inside.

'I love you, Rosalie Winters. I want you for my wife.' His lips quirked up in a smile that looked painfully tight. 'I want an affair with you that will last our whole lives.'

She stared. She'd seen his lips form the words. She'd *heard* the words. But they couldn't be right.

'There's no need to lie, Arik. There's no need to be gallant.'

'Gallant? To my shame, that's one thing I haven't been with you, *habibti*. I've been short-sighted, selfish. A slave to desire.' His hands pulled her close, sliding restlessly over her in long, urgent caresses that moulded her to his hard length.

'I thought I knew what I wanted. Thought I knew it all. What a fool I was!' He lowered his head to nuzzle her cheek,

her ear, caress her neck with his lips till her head swam and
darts of sweet sensation jetted through her. 'I had no idea.
None at all.'

'You love me?' The words finally emerged from her
rusty throat.

'I *adore* you, Rosalie. Your passion, your beauty, your seductive body. But so much more than that. It's your spirit, your
stubborn, gritty, honest strength of character.' He pulled back
just far enough to look her in the eye and what she saw in his
face made her blink.

'You're beautiful on the inside as well as the outside. I've
never met a woman like you. So gentle, clever and patient. So
strong. I planned to seduce you into my life but it was you
who did the seducing. I couldn't get you out of my mind. Even
when you ran away. Even when I discovered who you were.
I was honour-bound to leave you alone and yet still I couldn't
turn from you as I should.'

His eyes, blazing with dark fire, held hers and, despite her
caution and her distrust, a tiny flare of excitement flickered
to life in the frozen recesses of her heart.

'What I feel is stronger than duty or honour. It has nothing
to do with shabby gossip or convenience.'

Rosalie's heart was doing somersaults in her chest. Her
whole body shook as she strove to understand. To be sensible.

'But you don't want a wife.'

'I didn't *plan* to take a wife yet. I was content with my
life as it was. Until I met you. You turned my world upside
down.' His caresses grew slower, his voice deeper, and
Rosalie's body responded immediately. She felt as if she
were melting.

'I wanted you for sex,' he whispered in a voice that rumbled,
low and seductive, right through her. 'I thought I knew how it
would be between us, Rosalie. But I was wrong. It was you
who taught me. About honesty and about a yearning stronger

even than lust. About love. Being with you was so different from being with any other woman.'

The weighted heat of his hands on her body drew the last of her strength away, lulling her into ecstasy and submission. But still she resisted.

'No! I'm just a novelty to you. That's all. I'm different to the other women you've…had.' He'd probably revelled in his role of teacher, in her patent lack of sensual knowledge. No wonder he was intrigued. But that would pass.

His hands tightened almost painfully. 'Is your self-confidence so bruised that you actually believe that?'

Rosalie shook her head, denying the temptation of his words. It couldn't be true. It couldn't. Why was he so set on convincing her of something so patently impossible?

'You barely know me.' And yet that hadn't stopped her from falling head over heels in love with him.

'I know you, Rosalie. I know you enough to want to spend the rest of my life with you.'

The echo of his words thrummed in the silence between them and she let her eyes close, allowing herself the luxury of hope.

'But I understand it may be too soon for you, sweetheart. I will give you time.' He drew her so close that she was plastered against him, her head tucked into his chest so she could hear the heavy, rapid thump of his heart. Her whole body flush with his, his legs planted wide, surrounding her. It was heaven.

'You've been treated badly in the past. You have every reason not to trust. I understand that.' She felt the vibration of his voice rumble in his chest, heard its dark liquid tones, sweet as honey. 'And I've compounded your distrust, losing my temper, awakening old hurts. I can't expect you to love me—yet. But give us time, Rosalie. You'll see that I can be more than a lover. I'll make a good husband, a loving father for Amy.'

*Amy.* Rosalie sucked in a deep breath redolent with his warm, spicy scent as his words struck her. He wanted to be a father to Amy! To a child whose biological father was unknown: a cowardly, violent abuser.

Arik was willing to commit himself to taking on her daughter in such circumstances?

In a country where traditions of birthright and lineage and honour were so strong, he wanted to father her little girl.

Rosalie lifted her head, blinking up at him through the sudden glaze of hot tears.

'You want to be a father to Amy?'

'Of course. She is a part of you. And she's special in her own right. So bright, so beautiful, so…Rosalie! What is it? Don't cry, my little rose. Don't cry, please.' He rocked her close against him, so close they were melded together. 'Whatever it is, I'll make it right. I swear it.'

She shook her head, knowing suddenly that it *was* right. So perfect that it was better even than her secret fantasies. What daydream could match the reality of Arik's love? So real and warm and full that she felt as if her heart were overflowing.

She rose on tiptoe, pulling his head down towards her so she could press her lips against his.

Instantly his mouth took hers, delving deeply, thoroughly in a sensuous kiss that spoke of barely restrained passion, soul-deep yearning. His embrace was possessive, almost too tight as he held her close. His body was locked hard with banked emotion, with a desire that matched her own. She felt his rigid erection against her belly and pressed up against it.

Arik shuddered, hauling her closer, hands splayed over her bottom as he shifted his weight, aligning them more intimately. The heat between them was volcanic, sparking and alive. She pressed into him and heard him groan.

'No, Rosalie. We mustn't.' He pressed his forehead against hers as he sucked in breaths so deep his chest heaved. 'Not here, not now.'

'I love you, Arik,' she whispered unsteadily.

'Rosalie!' His hand under her chin tilted her head so she met his blazing eyes. 'What did you say?'

'I love you.' She smiled through tears of happiness. 'I've loved you from the first, didn't you know? That's why I ran away. I couldn't bear to think you only wanted—'

'Shh, little one. Don't say it. Don't remind me of how shallow I was.' But already, as the stern control slid away from his features, she read the sensual intent there. The hawk-eyed intensity that told her just what he had on his mind.

He stepped forward, backing her up against the wall. 'So, you will marry me?' His hands caressed her slowly, sending delicious thrills of desire right through her. She caught her breath at the waves of sensation coiling already in the pit of her stomach.

'Say it, Rosalie. Say you'll marry me.'

That was when she saw it. The tiniest trace of uncertainty, of doubt, in his face. As if he, too, needed reassurance. She reached up and clasped his warm cheeks in her shaking hands.

'You're the only man in the world I *could* marry, Arik. I love you so much.'

The rest of her words were cut off as his mouth took hers. Sensual heat flared instantly as he pushed her back against the wall, his body a seductive weight, his hands exploring each sensitive spot, slowing at the buttons on her shirt—

'Mummy!' Tiny hands tugged at her trousers and instantly, breathlessly, Arik stood back.

They stared at each other in shocked silence, knowing that in just a few minutes more her trousers would have been pooled around her ankles and his clothes discarded in a heap.

'Why are you kissing Arik, Mummy?'

Rosalie looked down into her daughter's curious face and knew one last hurdle remained. She reached down and pulled Amy into her arms.

'Because I love him, darling. And he loves me.' She held

her breath, aware of Arik's tense stance matching her own. 'He wants to be your daddy, Amy. He wants us to live with him.'

'Really?' Huge eyes turned from her to Arik and a trickle of fear slid down Rosalie's spine. How would she handle this if Amy couldn't cope with the idea?

'Really,' Arik's deep voice answered. 'I want you to be my little girl as well. We'll all be one family.'

'And G'anma?'

'And your grandma too.'

'And Auntie Belle and Uncle Rafi and Adham?'

'They're already my family, Amy.'

'Good. I like my family.' She stared up at Arik. 'I like you too.' She blew him a kiss. 'Can we have breakfast now? I'm hungry.'

Rosalie stifled a burble of hysterical laughter at the look on Arik's face. Nonplussed barely described it.

'You go on ahead, sweetie, and we'll follow.' She put Amy down and watched her head for the door.

'The final seal of approval,' he murmured, his lips twitching.

'Except for your own family,' she suddenly remembered.

He shook his head and reached out a hand to her cheek. Her eyes closed at the tender caress of his fingers against her sensitive flesh.

'Don't worry, little one. My mother's home from her apartment in Paris and she's eager to meet you. She's been hinting for ages that it's time I settled down with one woman, but I suspect it's your painting that's really intrigued her. She's seen it and she approves. She thinks that at last I'm showing some real discrimination, choosing an artist as my woman.'

'Really?'

'Yes, really.' His hand slid down the column of her throat to the throbbing pulse at its base, drawing tingling responses from her with every feather-light touch.

'You know,' he mused, 'I was so sure it would be safe to talk to you here, with Amy present.' His hand drew lower across her skin, down to the top button of her shirt. Immediately her nipples peaked in expectation.

'I thought I'd be able to keep my hands to myself, knowing she was here.'

'You proposed to me in a stable because you didn't trust yourself to be alone with me?' Rosalie didn't know whether to be amused or horrified.

'Of course.' One dark eyebrow winged up at her doubt. 'It seemed more sensible than finding a romantic spot where I might be tempted to seduce you.'

His fingers brushed the tiny buttons of her shirt, snaring the breath in her throat.

'But you're not tempted here?' Her voice was uneven, a dead giveaway to the excitement rocketing through her.

He shook his head, slipping a button undone and pressing his lips to her collar-bone. Rosalie sighed and let her head loll back against the wall, feeling the inevitable loosening of muscles as her body anticipated his.

'I'm *always* tempted by you, my sweet rose.' He lifted his head long enough to sear her with his gaze. 'We need to marry very soon.'

Wordlessly she nodded, already sliding into the beckoning heat of his caresses, of their mutual desire, knowing that, beyond all expectation, she was utterly secure in the arms of the man she loved.

'You are everything to me,' he murmured, his lips teasing her as he followed the trail of her buttons, popping each one open. His breath hazed her skin and she reached for him, holding him as if she'd never let him go.

'Amy might come back,' she croaked as his mouth closed on her breast and she arched up against him.

'Rafiq will stop her. My cousin's no fool.' With a quick, deft movement Arik flicked open her bra and tugged it out of the way. His mouth on her bare flesh made her writhe.

'They're expecting us for breakfast,' she gasped.

'Later.' He smoothed his broad hands over her torso and down to the waistband of her trousers. She felt his smile against her breast. 'Breakfast can wait.'

0807/06

# FREE

## 4 BOOKS AND A SURPRISE GIFT!

We would like to take this opportunity to thank you for reading this Mills & Boon® book by offering you the chance to take FOUR more specially selected titles from the Modern™ series absolutely FREE! We're also making this offer to introduce you to the benefits of the Mills & Boon® Reader Service™—

- ★ **FREE home delivery**
- ★ **FREE gifts and competitions**
- ★ **FREE monthly Newsletter**
- ★ **Books available before they're in the shops**
- ★ **Exclusive Reader Service offers**

Accepting these FREE books and gift places you under no obligation to buy; you may cancel at any time, even after receiving your free shipment. Simply complete your details below and return the entire page to the address below. You don't even need a stamp!

**YES!** Please send me 4 free Modern books and a surprise gift. I understand that unless you hear from me, I will receive 6 superb new titles every month for just £2.89 each, postage and packing free. I am under no obligation to purchase any books and may cancel my subscription at any time. The free books and gift will be mine to keep in any case.

P7ZEE

Ms/Mrs/Miss/Mr.............................Initials .................................
BLOCK CAPITALS PLEASE

Surname ...................................................................................

Address ...................................................................................

...............................................................................................

....................................................Postcode ..............................

Send this whole page to:
The Reader Service, FREEPOST CN81, Croydon, CR9 3WZ